NEAR DEATH

Near Death
First Edition August 2022
Edited By: Wendy Maynard
Cover Illustration By: A. A. Medina |
Fabled Beast Designs

NEAR DEATH

STEPHEN COOPER

Splatploitation Press

Katie and Ditch

A thick rusty chain bolted to a grey cellar wall led to a dirty female foot laying on threadbare sheets. A worn leather strap at the end of the chain clutched tightly around her ankle. The metal silver buckle to the strap dug viciously into the red raw skin underneath it. A slight movement of the foot showed the extent of the rubbing as an inch of skin above and below the strap had been scraped away. Dry blood caked the black strap and flickers of crimson remained ingrained in the links of the slightly discoloured chain.

One of her toes was missing. The fourth toe on her right foot. Its absence was replaced by nothing more than a badly healed stub that looked infected. The other toes hadn't fared much better, but at least remained in place. However, all were missing their toenails. None of the toenails had fallen off in any natural way, they'd all been yanked off to great pain, or pleasure, depending on the perspective within the heinous act. Hints of toenail growing back had started to sprout, but for the moment, bruised exposed skin mixed with the filth exuding from her unwashed foot.

Cigarette burns were dotted all the way up both her formerly beautiful legs, the smoothness a distant memory as flakes of skin dripped from the repeatedly melted limbs. More dirt and blood added an extra almost permanent layer to the legs and doubled up as a form of glue holding what remained of the skin in place. Blisters and bruises hid camouflaged amongst the grime as well as a collection of fresh and healed cuts.

At the top of her legs, a tattered grey skirt hung loosely from her thin waist. She wasn't quite emaciated yet, but had begun showing signs of heading in that direction after always being considered a healthy-looking girl in the past. Her underwear was long gone. Ripped from her the day she arrived. It now resided as a trophy for her captor somewhere outside of the cellar.

Two more chains stretched to her body holding both arms in place. Much like her ankles circles of raw skin hid under the beefy straps. The left strap looked significantly newer than the right with blood only just starting to discolour it, while the right strap had been lapping it up for years. Unlike her toes, all her fingers remained attached for now, and while her fingernails were all cracked, none were missing. They weren't in a great state. But in comparison to her feet, they'd definitely suffered a lot less.

The girl's skinny gaunt stomach was badly scarred. Most were crudely healed, but one appeared fresh. Blood still trickled from the slice across her lower abdomen, although the main gush had now passed. As her body twisted slightly upwards some of the remaining blood spilled back into her belly button. The rest nestled next to small mounds of dry blood protruding from her abused stomach. A ripped crop top hid the bite marks and cigarette burns that plastered her tits. A little modesty remained, if such a laughable thing existed in this foul place. The top itself told a story. The formerly white top was now a mixture of red and brown, while the one remaining frail strap was ready to snap at any given moment. A small microcosm of its owner.

Beads of a feverish sweat dripped from her neck on to the flimsy top. She had been regularly dosed up with antibiotics during her stay in the fiendish cellar, but they could only do so much. Some droplets stayed next to the strangle marks that ran loops around the circumference of her neck. They glistened within the dark marks underneath them. She'd lost count of how many times she'd been strangled, of how many times she'd been near death. The job was never quite finished, but evidences of the cruel act remained. It was a shock it hadn't caused some kind of permanent brain damage yet, although the mental toll it had taken could easily qualify in that department.

Then there was her face. Once upon a time she'd be described as cute, but little of that fresh-faced innocence had survived. Katie was in her mid-twenties, looked young for her age they used to say, but you wouldn't be able to tell anymore. Both her eyes were badly swollen to the point of barely being able to open them, not that she'd want to. Her nose was broken and unlikely to ever be set right. It wasn't quite question mark shaped yet but the next blow it took would probably send it that way. Her lips were dry and repeated cuts on them had left permanent scars. She was missing two teeth as well. The second of which she had no recollection of how it was lost. The first happened the day she arrived.

Clumps of sweaty hair stuck to her forehead. The top of her head could be labelled as patchy at best. Large amounts of hair had been ripped from the roots and torn away with a slim chance of it growing back. Her long fluffy brown hair used to be the thing she liked most about herself, now little of it remained. She hated every part of her abused wrecked body. Katie was grateful at this point she hadn't seen herself in a mirror since her arrival. The man responsible had teased that one day he'd roll in a full length mirror so she could witness the little that remained of her. So far that had just been a threat, unlike every other nasty remark that he'd fully followed through on.

Ditch leaned over her face reapplying her make-up. Some cruel joke about keeping her pretty, though that ship had sailed. Katie highly doubted she could ever look pretty again with the horrors she'd already endured. His hand was steady and calm as he applied a dark red lipstick to her swollen and shredded lips. Each stroke stung more than the last. She couldn't scream, or try and shake him away, as that would result in something much worse than the stinging of her lips. She would know, Katie was now a veteran at being tortured.

Ditch was in his early forties. Long greasy hair hung from his face, grey before its time. His eyes were a piercing brown and stuck from his face in an almost googly-eyed fashion. The rest of his face had a plainness to it, nothing remarkable. If it wasn't for those eyes you could pass this guy in the street and think nothing of him, but those eyes really were a memorable feature. Doubly so for all his female victims across the last two decades.

He wore a boiler suit that housed various rags sticking from the pockets. He had on a red one today, brown the day before. Fortunately the colour change was because it was a different suit rather than more sinister reasons - not that these suits hadn't seen every wicked act known to man. They'd all been covered in so many different girls' blood, piss, and shit, that Ditch had to rotate the suits regularly to keep them from smelling horrendous or falling apart. He had three suits in total. It was the blue one's turn in a few days if Katie didn't cover the red one in blood beforehand. Obviously that one hid the stains the best. Still, Ditch liked to keep them relatively clean, he enjoyed seeing blood more than being covered in it.

Ditch had abandoned his real name a long time ago. He took up the name Ditch some twenty years beforehand when he first started his savagery. It was a way of making him the man he was today. Of marking a new beginning that changed him from some bitter unfulfilled pathetic warehouse worker to the cruel bastard and king of his own domain he was now.

He thought up the name when burying his first victim. Shallow Grave seemed like too much of a code name, so Ditch would suffice he thought while barely burying a ravaged teenage girl. She was the first of many victims that came long before the setup he had now. Back then he was more of a drag them in the woods and rape and murder them type of killer, rather than the more calculated and somewhat cautious approach he took to the act now. He'd matured.

Ditch was a physically strong guy, but you wouldn't think it to look at him. Much of his strength was hidden away with his frame looking slight to outsiders. Five percent body fat told a different story. He wasn't a gym bunny or anything like that, just always on the move. Always active. Always plotting and scheming and behaving deplorably. It turned out kidnapping and torturing people was an extremely effective workout regime.

Katie turned her head slightly away from Ditch as he finished applying the lipstick. Luckily, the movement wasn't enough to be considered disrespectful and earn her a punch. More like her head had fallen to the side as she lapsed in and out of consciousness, which is exactly what had happened. It had become a regular occurrence since her stay in the cellar. Sometimes Ditch punished her for it, sometimes he let it slide. Kept her on her toes, so to speak. This time he allowed it, but next time it could easily result in him using a blowtorch on her.

On the other side of the thin but reinforced bed to Ditch sat another figure in the room. This one hid in the shadows that dominated that side of the cellar past Katie's bed. He wore a long black cloak barely visible against the grey concrete wall where the beginnings of Katie's chains were housed. The cloak blended into the shadows, along with the rest of the mysterious figure. The only thing that ever seemed remotely visible about the ambiguous man was his rotten teeth. Not that Ditch ever paid any attention to them. They seemed purely for Katie to focus on when the pain got too much. She knew things were absolutely fucking dire when a pair of decaying teeth were her escape.

The figure always quietly watched Katie from the safety of the shadows. He never dared to step forth and incur Ditch's wrath as well. The figure hadn't spoken to Katie since her arrival either, just watched. Always watching. Surveying the various inflictions of torment from the shadows. A willing spectator to Ditch's cruelty. As far as Katie was concerned he was just as guilty as Ditch. Anyone who could stand by and watch this punishment without so much as raising a single concern was clearly a fucking evil cunt too. She'd begged for his help when she first arrived, but had long since given up pleading.

Ditch briefly moved away from Katie as some consciousness returned to her. He snatched a nearby Polaroid camera and quickly made his return beaming down at her made-up face. Grabbing her by the cheeks he angled Katie's face back up towards him and the camera. The lipstick, mascara, and blush did little to hide her swollen eyes and cut lips. No amount of make-up could ever cover her brutalised face. Ditch didn't mind though, he still liked the tease of it. The illusion that the make-up could somehow help hide the punishment he'd dealt. He leaned in snapping a close-up that momentarily brightened the dimly lit cellar as the flash popped.

"There we go. Beautiful again," Ditch taunted as he discarded the make-up from the bed into Katie's bag, although she didn't really consider it hers bag anymore. He stole it when he first brought her here and had rummaged through it so many times that any essence of it belonging to her was long gone. It was his now. He told her that once and she nodded in agreement. There was no point arguing, he was right. He also told her she belonged to him as well. That one she did argue, and lost a toe for it.

Ditch began to shake the Polaroid as the image started to develop. He wandered to a white board located at the far side of the room careful to avoid the two buckets resting next to Katie's bed. Both rested on newspaper that contained articles of a manhunt to find her, and a story about a discovered body of the missing girl's boyfriend. He'd read the articles aloud to her with great amusement when he first got them. Over and over. She cried every time, and he punished her for the tears every time. Afterwards he decided they'd make a good under layer for the shit bucket he used when wiping the crap from the bed. That made him chuckle, and resulted in him giving Katie a black eye when she didn't join in the laughter. Stupid cunt's fault for not having a sense of humour.

The shit bucket was one of the first tools he used to break the girls when he brought them back to the cellar. When they needed the toilet he'd lay a bent metal sheet under their bodies that then angled down to the buckets. They then had to piss or shit on to the sheet that slid the excrement to the bucket, or they could lay in their own filth. The choice was theirs, although Ditch much preferred them to use the sheet and bucket as it kept the smell to a more reasonable level. Luckily for him after much protest and embarrassment they always did end up using the sheet and bucket. He trained them well.

Ditch reached the board and pinned the exposed Polaroid somewhere in the middle of a list of thirty-plus women. He wrote the number ten beside it indicating how many days Katie had been in the cellar. All the other names had pictures and numbers alongside them as well. The pictures all contained brutalised women, Ditch's victims. None of them where here now however, they'd all died horrible deaths along the way. Every girl now rested in an unmarked burial ground not far from the cellar, but away from civilisation and the possibility of ever being discovered. Katie was the latest in line, and according to the board, she'd survived longer than a fair few of them, but still had a long way to go until she reached the top of the so-called 'leader board.'

"You're doing well," Ditch acknowledged as he stared at the board. It was his pride and joy. Everything else in the cellar may have been covered in blood, and shit, and fuck knows what else, but the board was kept out of the firing line and as clean as possible. Even Ditch tended to wipe his hands on his various rags before using it for fear of smudging the black marker names or dirtying the photos. He'd shown the board more care on any given day than he had every woman he'd ever met in his entire life put together.

Katie didn't hear his encouragement. She'd faded into unconsciousness once more as she remained chained and strapped to the old bed. Her scarred and battered body laying above the mangy sheets. Ditch's eyes left her for a moment and settled on a table occupying the wall to his side. On it rested a host of potential weapons ranging from garden tools to actual weapon weapons. They were all out of Katie's reach, but not Ditch's.

Before The Cellar

A beat-up old Pontiac Fiero overlooked the exquisite countryside from its hill top vantage point as the last remnants of the sun slowly faded from view. The night-time air remained warm in the sun's impending absence as Katie and Ryan sat atop the old car's roof watching the final rays disappear. Well, Katie watched the sunset. Ryan's eyes were on something he considered far more beautiful than any picturesque sunset could ever be - Katie.

Beautiful long brown hair framed Katie's youthful face. Her chubby cheeks added to the young look but also gave her an extra measure of prettiness in Ryan's eyes. High cheekbones did it for him. Despite being twenty-five Katie still got ID'd for absolutely everything. Her wide bright eyes didn't help her in that department either adding to the fresh-faced look, but they did help her every other way as Ryan regularly got lost in them. He was truly mesmerised by her.

She wore a white crop top and a short grey skirt. If anyone was looking up at the car roof from the bonnet they'd easily get an eyeful of her underwear but no one was around for miles. Plus Katie didn't care. She liked dressing a little bit promiscuously, especially when it wasn't obvious at first glance. She'd often wear something that looked perfectly normal but then catch Ryan out by showing him between her legs while she read a book or bent over to get something from a draw. It was her way of playfully teasing him. A private joke between them.

Ryan was a couple of years older than Katie. While she looked young for her age he'd regularly get mistaken for being much older than his years. They often joked about Ryan being a cradle snatcher despite the relatively small age gap. Ryan was a good foot taller than her which also added to the illusion. It wasn't like Katie was short, he was just tall standing easily above six feet. He was athletic with the kind of face you'd see attached to any former jock in a high school movie. Rugged good looks, Katie would say, but not Ryan. Despite his good looks and athletic build, he was a humble person. A shy guy in a popular guy's body. It was one of the many, many things Katie loved about him. He truly was a gentle giant and an extremely sweet one at that.

Both held a glass of wine in their hands as they sat on the car roof. The roof moaned a little under their combined weight, mostly Ryan's rather than Katie's, but them sitting on the car was the least of its worries. One of the reasons they'd stopped at the beautiful hillside rest stop was to give the car a break after steam started to pour from the engine. While the warm air enhanced their day it had given the old car all sorts of problems. It was the latest in a long line of mechanic faults that had begun to ring up quite the repair bill, a lot more than the car was worth.

Ryan loved the car, it had served him well, but he was never one to get too attached and nostalgic about material things. He cared about flesh and blood, about friendships and the important people in his life. He knew the car's time was finally up. In fact, plans were already in place to replace it by the end of the month. It had been nice to take the car out on one more journey though, even if it did require more pit stops than travelling with a toddler.

Katie's eyes left the sunset and settled on the small picnic they'd laid out on the car bonnet after the engine had cooled. It was silly really, they'd only packed a couple of rolls and a bottle of wine that was meant to be a gift, but now it had become a picnic. It was laid out like they'd gone for a day in the countryside. In retrospect they kind of had, but that wasn't the initial plan. They'd originally set off to see a friend on the other side of the country but the trip had been cancelled last minute. So last minute in fact that they were on their way there when Katie received the phone call.

She was fuming at their flaky friend for cancelling last second after taking time off work to come and see him, but Ryan was far too laid back to get stressed over something like that. Turning off the motorway he decided a drive through the countryside was in order. Maybe they could find a bed and breakfast too if the mood took them and devise their own trip instead. They had the best part of a week free to themselves now so why not? He was always the optimistic type. Never let a day go to waste.

Staring at the food Katie noticed a few cakes and packets of crisps had found their way into the picnic. Ryan always snuck in more food when Katie wasn't looking. It was always cake and crisps too. He would live of the stuff if he could. He had a snack cupboard back at their small apartment that always appeared full despite him regularly visiting it. The number of times she'd caught him having a lemon slice or angel cake for breakfast was ridiculous. It did make her laugh and smile every time though, especially when he pulled that 'caught raiding the cookie jar face.'

Katie cuddled up to Ryan with a massive smile spread across her face. He returned kind. Their arms interlocked as they rested their heads on each other, something they often did. Their friends always joked they were one of those couples that were sickeningly cute together. They wore it as a badge of honour.

"Love you," Katie told Ryan as they remained entangled.

"Love you too," he replied, kissing the tip of her nose just as she liked.

They both sat intertwined as they watched the vivid moon take hold of the sky away from the glare of city lights. Katie daydreamed about the life ahead of them, and all the lovely adventures they could go on, while Ryan lived in the moment and thought about nothing more than having Katie in his arms. Katie nuzzled further into Ryan and could feel his smile grow as he smelt her fluffy beautiful hair as she rested on his shoulder.

Ryan tried to take a sip of his wine without unlocking their arms, not wanting to spoil the moment. It didn't go well. Katie couldn't help but burst out laughing as he spilt the red wine all down his favourite t-shirt. Luckily he'd managed to miss her as Katie pre-emptively moved back as he drew the glass to his lips. In hindsight she may have even been the cause for the mishap. Either way the important thing was Ryan didn't spill red wine over her lovely white top.

As Ryan began to pat his top dry Katie reached for a roll and stuffed it into his mouth causing her to laugh even harder. Ryan leant forward to kiss the mischievous vixen with the roll still sticking from his mouth. Katie playfully batted him away before succumbing to his advances and kissing him back with the roll stuck between their lips. Katie took a bite but had to spit it out as she was laughing to hard and almost fell off the roof while somehow not choking. She kept her balance as Ryan gently seized her arm. He couldn't have loved her more in that moment if he tired. She was his everything.

With the roll out the way the two kissed again under the moonlight. Ryan's hand played with Katie's hair as he drew her closer to his body. She pressed her hand against his shoulder and tenderly stroked it in kind. Their mouths locked together with no thought of ever parting. Ryan's hand slid from her hair to meet Katie's other hand down by her side. His large fingers sweetly rubbed her index finger, a sign of affection he'd only ever used on her, and only ever would. It felt like a magical moment for them both as they sat together kissing on top of the old car under the charming moonlit sky in the bewitching countryside, although most moments felt this way when they were together.

Ryan continued to softly rub her finger as they kissed. Katie's other hand left his shoulder searching further down his body as she reached his jeans. He was hard for her, always was whenever they kissed. Four years together hadn't changed that, and no amount of time afterwards would either. She rubbed his cock through his jeans and began to slowly unzip them. Ryan's free hand unhooked her bra in one easy movement and discarded it somewhere on the car roof. He'd gotten good at that, Katie thought as she remembered how much he used to fidget trying to get it off. Running her fingers over his dick she wondered whether the car rooftop could handle them making love on top of it.

They'd never find out though as Ditch silently approached them with a heavy duty pipe wrench in hand and both of them unaware of his wicked presence.

No Smiling

Katie's mouth morphed into a rare smile as she lay asleep chained to the uncomfortable bed in the dank cellar. Her swollen eyelids flickered as she dreamt of better times. Katie rubbed her thumb against her index finger on her left hand in a similar manner to what Ryan used to do making the chains rattle slightly under the gentle gesture. Ryan was her happy place, her escape from the despair and torture that had followed. But it was only an escape in her mind, physically she already knew she'd never leave this inhuman prison. Ditch knew it too.

He stood over her. Watched her sleep from a couple of metres away, but moved closer when he saw her smile and gauged the slight movement of the chains. Ditch's grubby hand darted towards Katie's fingers as he venomously seized her index finger while she continued to peacefully rub it eliciting her nostalgic smile further. The smile instantly faded as Ditch snapped her index finger back. Katie tried to scream but no sounds emerged from her mouth, such was the shock. Immediately awake, she had no fucking clue what had just happened until she peered down at her mangled finger that now pointed away from her and understood what the sickening crack sound was.

Before Katie could fully comprehend how it had happened Ditch slapped her hard across the face as he leered at her swollen confused eyes. "No smiling! You know the rules," he whooped as he slapped her again and spat in her face. Spit rolled from Katie's forehead onto the stinging red handprint left by the slap as she tried to reply. Another slap landed hard on her cheek wrenching her mouth to one side and sending her teeth grinding awkwardly against one another before she could question his actions.

"No smiling!" he screamed again as another weaker slap brushed across the top of her forehead swatting the remaining spit from her brow. He hadn't aimed the last slap, more just lashed out in a manic way to continue the torture. His grin gave away the fact that he wasn't actually in a frenzy at her apparent misbehaviour, he was just being a complete and utter dick, because he could be. Snapping her finger and giving her a couple of slaps while gobbing in her face was amusing to him. The no smile rule wasn't a thing, although after the fun he'd just had he did consider introducing it.

Not that the girls smiled much in the cellar. One or two of them would at the beginning. They'd try and charm their way out of the place by telling him that it wasn't too late to let them go, that they had rich daddies who would pay him for their release like it was a fucking hostage situation. A couple of others had offered those big fake Instagram smiles they believed would entice him to give them their freedom back after a good blowjob. Ditch didn't give a shit about blowjobs. He was a pussy and ass man.

If he wanted a blowjob he'd pull every single one of their teeth out and get one. No way was he risking his dick getting bitten off by some nasty cunt when he could take whatever he wanted anyway. They all soon realised the false smiles and big-eyed pleas weren't going to work. It normally happened after he cut something off. So while the no smiling rule was funny, it was also redundant.

Tears flowed freely from Katie's puffy eyes. The pain of the broken finger merged with the smarting from the slaps to pile on more misery. She glanced down at her index finger confirming it really was pointing in a completely different direction from all the others. She couldn't even reach across with her other hand to gently hold the bent finger and ease the discomfort with the chains offering no give. The finger just hung there. Katie wanted to scream and shout all kinds of abuse at her serial tormentor but knew that would just bring more suffering. That's how Ditch operated. The more you reacted and whined, the more abuse you received. She found that out the hard way several times over during the early days. The early days seemed like such a weird way of thinking when it had been less than two weeks, but those two weeks had felt like several long cruel lifetimes to Katie.

Katie's mind betrayed her as her eyes fell on the cellar door at the opposite end of the room next to the leader board. She couldn't make out any real details on the board with her eyes in the state they were, but the big brown door was easily identifiable. It sat there mocking her day after day. Every other moment in her life those few metres would be so easily reached, but now they felt like a mountain's climb away. The ultimate tease. Being able to see salvation, but not reach it.

She had no idea what awaited on the other side of the

door. Ditch hadn't given her any hint of where she was. Katie didn't know how long she had been unconscious in the pick-up and her brain was scrambled after seeing Ryan brutally killed anyway. She could be hundreds of miles away from that hilltop for all she knew. But whatever was on the other side of the door had to be better than what awaited her in the cellar. Better than the abuse, torture, and all the weapons ready to take their next pound of flesh. Better than Ditch and whatever next sadistic act he had planned for her. No matter where it led, it would at least get her further away from him.

Ditch followed her unintended stare at the door, his turn to smile now. "I told you about the last girl that tried to escape," he bragged. His eyes drifted to the cellar floor in between the bed and the doorway. They settled on a vile dark blood stain ingrained on the cellar's stone floor. A deep black hellish stain. "The one stain I've never managed to get out," he theatrically added with a devilish smile. He loved this memory, and any opportunity he got to talk about his previous conquest he would, especially his favourite one.

"Jasmine, her name was," he told Katie who already knew. This wasn't the first time Ditch had recounted the story to her. It was a cautionary tale he narrated to all newbies upon arrival. He retold how she somehow broke one of the straps holding her hands. "Purely by accident, so don't get any ideas," he said with a knowing grin, but it had snapped nonetheless. Ditch was out when it happened so Jasmine had time to unbind her other arm and free her legs. Just as she'd finished unchaining herself however the door opened. Ditch entered before she could even think to form an escape plan or grab a weapon to protect herself.

She had tried to plead with him, convince Ditch that the restraint had mysteriously snapped and she was simply stretching while she awaited his return. "She meant nothing by it!" Ditch mockingly mimicked to Katie while regurgitating Jasmine's lie. It wouldn't have mattered either way anyway. In Ditch's eyes any deviation from her being chained to the fucking bed amounted to an escape attempt. Treason in his mind, a crime of the highest order. The conniving bitch had to suffer. "She was doing well at the time too," Ditch informed Katie like that was something that really mattered. Like she was a contender. It would have mattered a great deal if the prize for first place was being released from this hellhole, but the actual prize for lasting the longest was that you'd suffered the most and would continue to endure more misery. Hardly a great incentive.

He told Katie once again in great detail how he broke every single bone in her body using a mallet. Even brought out the hammer to show her. It still had remnants of Jasmine's blood on the metal head he claimed. It definitely was blood-stained, but whether or not it was hers was anyone's guess, not even Ditch truly knew after how often he'd used it. But for the purpose of his story, he liked to believe it was Jasmine who forever stained it. A second everlasting stain, she deserved that honour.

Ditch's smirk grew off his face as he started excitingly

naming the bones he'd broken like some kind of biology professor. Occasionally he'd even break into song telling her what bone was connected to what. How a man like Ditch knew the name of all the bones was beyond Katie, but it wasn't exactly a question she could ask him. After he'd broken all two hundred and six bones he left Jasmine on the floor free of her restraints with the door wide open. He even went out for a while eventually bringing back some burgers for them both.

Needless to say, she hadn't budged an inch during his absence and couldn't eat a thing either. Jasmine just lay on the floor a crumbled broken mess waiting, and hoping, to die. It took another day for her to pass, although Ditch knew she wished it was instantaneous. Such was the spirit of the human mind though. That's why he enjoyed breaking it so much, it was the supreme challenge. Once you've broken that human spirit nothing else can compare with that buzz he cold-heartedly finished with as the retelling of Jasmine's plight for freedom came to an end.

Katie looked away from the insurmountable door rolling her head towards the figure on the other side of her instead. She wondered what his role had been in Jasmine's escape attempt. Did he just continue to sit there silently watching? Or had he been the one to break the strap? He didn't seem the sort to help in any way but Katie still didn't understand his role in any of this as he continued to watch from the shadows. Once again all she could really see of him was his rotten teeth. They seemed to be shaped in a smile after listening to Ditch recount his horrific story, but that could have just been Katie's imagination. As much as she wanted his help, she wanted to hate him just as much for not helping her. For being complicit in Ditch's heinous actions. However, as far as she knew he wasn't even in the room for Jasmine's escape attempt. Ditch never mentioned him despite going into excruciating detail about every other part of the morbid story.

Ditch dragged a stool to the middle of the cellar humming along to the bone rhyme now that it was stuck in his head. He opened a bag of mixed nuts and sat on the chair as he began munching on them. Ditch picked a chewed cashew from his mouth and threw it at the back of Katie's head. "Hey, look at me bitch."

Katie turned to face him. Not facing him would have resulted in him using the mallet that sat in his lap after his demonstration of what he'd done to Jasmine with it. Katie didn't want a recreation, it was much simpler to just oblige.

He threw another chewed nut at Katie's face as she looked towards him. Ditch smirked at her lack of reaction, obedient bitch. That was always a sure sign he was getting close to completely breaking them. He glanced back towards the leader board alongside the mythical door. Katie was still somewhere in the middle of the pack but now had a number twelve beside her name. Nearly two weeks in this unforgiving hell. "Pass Amy tomorrow," Ditch told her with another smirk on his face. Fake praise. Although real praise wouldn't have held any more value. Surviving his barbaric wretchedness wasn't an accomplishment, it was a curse. Purgatory.

Ditch stood from his seat leaving behind the mallet and nuts. He strutted towards the leader board putting on a show of his power and cockiness for Katie as he grabbed Amy's picture from the board cleaning his hands with one of the rags beforehand. She had been a few years younger than Katie, fresh out of university and about to start her life. The picture showed the young girl with dirty blond hair and a disfigured face that was once the envy of many. She had an eye missing and her nose was just a hole in her face. Her cheeks were ripped to shreds and her mouth smashed apart. Her last few days locked in the cellar hadn't been pleasant, not that the first ten had been a breeze, but Ditch really ramped up the ultra-violence in the last few. He forgot why now.

If Katie saw the picture she'd probably scream herself to death knowing that's what she had coming. Ditch considered showing her but thought he'd keep the potential upcoming punishments as a surprise. He licked Amy's face and pinned the photo back on the board. "She had spirit, that one," he announced much to Katie's chagrin. She needed him to shut the fuck up now, but he never did. Ditch loved the sound of his own voice, especially when talking about his crushing victories.

"They all had spirit," he further divulged as he ran his hand down the board. This time his strut led him back to Katie. He sat on the edge of the bed alongside her. "Until they didn't," he stated with the remark firmly aimed at Katie as he watched the helplessness on her face. Before saying any more he grabbed her broken index finger. This time he snapped it back into place which hurt just as much as the initial break. Katie's screams lead to a couple more sharp slaps before Ditch briefly left her bedside to retrieve his mallet.

Ryan's Death

Crack!

Katie and Ryan's kiss was broken apart at the exact same moment as Ryan's skull. Neither saw Ditch sneak towards the car, nor heard the swing of the massive heavy-duty pipe wrench. Katie had been more interested in unzipping Ryan's jeans, while Ryan had been more focused on letting her. The sickening thud of metal on bone lifted Ryan off the car roof and caused him to crash down the other side. His head jarred against Katie's upon the initial impact and had knocked her backwards chipping one of her front teeth. She couldn't work out what had happened at first. It felt like Ryan fucking head-butted her, but she knew that couldn't be the case.

She too had rolled backwards off the old car but landed dazed and confused by the rear wheels while Ryan was to the side of the Fiero. Peering blurry-eyed underneath the car Katie spotted a pair of heavy work boots circle round the opposite end of the vehicle and she became aware they'd been attacked. She noticed Ryan lying still on the stoney ground near her with his eyes rolled back in his head, and she thought he was already dead. Blood cascaded down the side of his face from a coin sized hole in his fractured skull. His outstretched rigid legs pointed towards her while his bloody head lay paralysed next to the dusty front tires.

Katie tried getting to her feet desperate to reach Ryan

and make sure he was ok even though he couldn't possibly be. As she began the wobbly ascent she saw the work boots pass Ryan and stalk in her direction. Ditch appeared in front of Katie just as she'd reached her knees. He wore a stained blue boiler suit and held the wrench over his shoulder looking like some kind of deranged mechanic. If they had called the breakdown service for the steaming Fiero they wouldn't have imagined in their wildest nightmares this hulking piece of shit turning up. Even in her muddled state, she caught wind of Ditch's cold eyes almost sticking from his face as they stared through his long greasy hair. He was an evil Katie hadn't known existed.

An unholy smirk stretched across his twisted face seeing her in such a vulnerable position. He raised the mammoth wrench high in the air like he was ready to deliver the killer blow to the helpless and disorientated girl as she braced for impact. Katie thought it was the end, there was fuck all she could do to protect herself, but Ditch was just messing with her.

"Not yet," he told her as he freed one of his hands from the wrench. Ditch jabbed Katie solidly across the jaw with the free hard making sure to pull his powerful punch a little, but not a lot. He definitely wanted to hurt the bitch, just not kill her.

Katie slammed on to the ground hitting her head firmly on the car before she reached the deck. Between the punch, the car, and the landing, she'd become even more dazed. This time as she lay on the floor she couldn't move. Her body had given up on her. She just had to watch from her new clearer vantage point as Ditch made his way back to Ryan seemingly forgetting about her for the moment. Her eyes kept fading but she tried to stay conscious. She needed to keep aware of what was going on if they had any hope of getting out of this. She didn't realise at the time how naive that thinking was. There was no way out of this.

Ditch stood over Ryan who was still out cold from the initial whack. Ditch hadn't taken any chances. Ryan looked kind of geeky but Ditch was no fool. He saw the size of the lad and the love he had for his girl and knew the prick would put up a fight. So Ditch didn't let him. He almost knocked his fucking head off with that one full nasty swing of the solid metal wrench. He'd felt the vibration ring through the wrench such was the brutal impact. The fact that Ditch could see Ryan still faintly breathing proved his point. The kid was made of sterner stuff. Not that it mattered.

This time when Ditch raised the pipe wrench above his head he didn't take a hand off it. Instead he brought both hands viciously down cracking Ryan's skull further with a second blow. Then a third. Then a fourth. And a fifth. He fucking went nuts on the kid. Fragments of skull flew off the wrench each time he raised it. The silver metal turned a dark red as all sorts of brain matter and facial features covered it. The sixth shot squished one of Ryan's loose eyeballs and it now hung from a big screw towards the end of the pipe wrench like gum on a shoe.

Eight shots in total all connected with Ryan's skull and face. Ditch glanced over to see if Katie was still watching. The tears streaming from her eyes and wails emitting from her shocked mouth confirmed she was. 'Good,' he smiled. He swung the monstrous wrench like a golf club into Ryan's dead head one final time. That shot was purely for her, just to prove what a sick fuck he was, although she'd already got that message. The first blow proved that.

Ryan died somewhere between the second and third blow. He hadn't regained any sense of consciousness after the first strike, that in itself had caused irreparable brain damage that Ryan would never have recovered from, but Ditch wasn't taking any chances. Not that the beatdown afterwards was inspired by concern of Ryan getting back up. It was about having a laugh. It wasn't often Ditch attacked guys so he made sure to enjoy himself whenever he did.

Ditch hadn't been sure how the so-called fight with Ryan would go when he first saw him. He knew the second he laid eyes on Katie he had to have her, but normally he picked targets who were alone. Ones he'd scoped out for a while. He especially didn't tend to pick girls sitting next to someone the size of a fucking wrestler. What followed had almost been an indulgence for Ditch. Going medieval on someone with a pipe wrench wasn't the norm even for someone as fucked up and psychotic as Ditch but he just let his creative side take over.

He'd maybe killed three other guys in his lifetime and like Ryan, they were all men that had gotten in his way.

They'd been an obstacle rather than anything more delightful. He enjoyed the kill, but it wasn't the same as what he had in store for Katie. Killing Ryan was simply a way to get to her. It wasn't like he was going to step aside and let Ditch have his sick twisted way with his girl, so the fucker had to die. Really it was Katie's fault he was dead, Ditch reflected. Not that he gave a shit. He didn't have any moral code about killing dudes, they just weren't his type. He much preferred his long drawn-out process of taking the lives of women, that was his jam.

Ditch took a moment to gather his breath as swinging the heavy pipe wrench that hard had left him puffing. He was in good shape, but anyone who's been in a fight knows it takes it out of you, even if you're the one causing all the damage. He took a few deep breaths while smiling at Katie who remained on the floor in utter despair and disbelief at the repulsive impossible view in front of her. Ditch's face was caked in Ryan's blood with chunks of his inwards stuck to Ditch's greasy hair. The car was splattered with an unfeasible amount of blood too which also stretched to the stones and grass around them due to the cast-off from the wrench. The picturesque view ruined by an obvious ferocious crime scene.

He held a finger up to Katie indicating he'd be back for her in just one minute. Ditch grabbed Ryan's right arm and began to drag him towards the edge of the hill as Ryan's prone dead body scraped against the loose stones hidden in the grass while Ditch tugged him the short distance. He grabbed a roll with his free hand as he passed the car bonnet and stuffed it down his throat. It didn't seem to matter to Ditch that the roll was covered in Ryan's blood and was probably coated with brain gunk as well.

Ditch wasn't a cannibal or anything as fucked up and nasty as that, but for the most part, he wasn't the most hygienic either. He was just hungry, and a nice ham, cheese, and blood roll seemed to be in order. He would grab himself some cake on the way back, he thought as he gazed at the options. A nice slice of angel cake he concluded, not being a fan of lemon. A blood and brain roll was one thing, but fucking lemon!

Katie's sobs faded into a slight whimper as she softly cried out for Ryan before stopping altogether as she lapsed out of consciousness. Ditch informed her the lad couldn't hear her anymore just as she passed out. Just as well really, as Ditch pulled the remains of Ryan's ear off and tossed it at her to 'help out' with Ryan hearing Katie. She missed his hysterical laughter afterwards. She also missed Ditch kicking Ryan off the edge of the steep hill making his body a lot harder to find despite the very obvious indications from all the surrounding blood that he was dead. Ditch dusted off his hands, job done.

Now it was time to deal with the girl, after some lovely angel cake and maybe another roll.

Near Death

Ditch perched on the stool with a pair of dripping bloody pliers hanging loosely in his hand. His gaze was fixated on Katie's foot and the gap where her toe used to be. The second recently removed toe lay as a grisly mess on the bed carelessly tossed aside from Katie's mangled foot. The fresh wound was anything but stemmed. Blood and pus seeped from the newly made hole and dripped onto the rags that barely qualified as bed sheets even before getting covered in more gore. The removed toe was the toe beside Katie's big one this time, giving Katie's right foot a bird-like appearance. Not that you could tell that through all the red.

A pool of sweat circled Katie's head on the flimsy pillow. She lay asleep, or more accurately passed out, after the pain from the snipped off toe became too much. Katie had become upset once again thinking about Ryan's gruesome death and began screaming abuse at Ditch. The word 'bastard' was used on multiple occasions and she'd thrown a few 'cunts' in there too. Ditch put a stop to her hysterics the only way he knew how, the fun way too, in his opinion. He warned her that if she didn't shut the fuck up she'd lose something but that only heightened Katie's outburst as she informed Ditch she'd already lost everything. He begged to differ and took a toe showing her she still had plenty he could take. Eighteen digits still remained as Ditch sat ominously watching her contemplating taking another. Ater all, what's one more?

Katie tried to curl up in her pain induced sleep but the chains prevented the more comforting position jerking her back and keeping her from bringing her knees to her chest. The bonds tightening brought a new grin to Ditch's face. He wouldn't even allow her a moment of solace in her nightmarish sleep after hacking off a toe because she was in distress over her dead boyfriend who he'd savagely murdered. He really was every bit the sadistic cunt she'd accused him of being and wouldn't change it for the world.

She began to shiver as the chains strained once again sending her remaining teeth chattering together while more blood discharged from her deformed foot. Ditch scooted the stool a little closer. He leaned forward and watched her screwed up bloated eyes as they fluttered in some kind of state of shock. Maybe the blood lost was too much? Katie's whole body seemed on the verge of shutting down and he knew her mind was already in severe distress. Ditch sat intoxicated by Katie's near demise as he awaited his latest triumph, the moment his victim gave in and finally fucking died.

His eyes flicked back to the leader board and Katie's latest position. She sat a really respectable eighth on the board having survived two whole gruelling weeks. A fine effort indeed, Ditch thought as his mind briefly wondered to what type of girl he would bring here next. The girl before Katie had been a shy timid thing and the one before that didn't get out the starting blocks. She may have well just died in the fucking car journey with how little time it took to break her. Ditch fancied someone tougher next.

Maybe some hotshot with wild ambitions. Someone with something to really live for.

Katie had been by chance. Normally his abductions involved more pre-planning and had some design to them, a little more foresight. Katie however was just in the wrong place at the wrong time, and that little slutty display of hers on the car roof sealed the deal. He had to have her. More so, he had to break her. Ditch had set off that faithful morning to capture a completely different girl but it hadn't worked out and the chance was gone. Sometimes fate intervened like that. But in a cruel twist for Katie, Ditch spotted her on the long drive back. When God closes a door but opens a window, or whatever the bullshit saying was Ditch thought while watching her whoring it up on the car roof with the oversized jock.

She'd been fun too after the initial screaming, nonstop crying, and endless fucking whining. Afterwards he'd been able to gleefully torture her every day and she'd taken it like a champ. At times there would be the odd outpouring but mostly Katie was numb to Ditch's torment, and he liked that. Believed it gave her a chance of getting all the way to the top. Finally someone to outlast the incomparable Daisy. That one had fought him every step of the way, the buzz he felt finally breaking her had been orgasmic. Literally. He came in his boiler suit the moment she finally gave in and died like a good little cunt without him so much as touching his cock.

He hadn't committed some wild act that finally killed her either. She wasn't bleeding out from being sawn in half or anything as barbaric as that. She had simply finally given in, her mind had had enough. He'd tortured her to the point that even someone as strong-willed and ironclad as Daisy had given up and let herself drift away forever. Fuck, he loved that feeling. He lived for it, while they died for it.

Ditch's hopes that Katie would finally be the one to outlast Daisy had faded throughout the day. He'd began to realise she didn't have it in her, that she was still too cut up from the loss of that prick boyfriend of hers. Fuck that guy. She belonged to him now, and he had a different life in mind for her, albeit a short one. One of unrelenting torture and overwhelming pain that eventually death would release her from, which incidentally would make him feel more alive. The circle of life. Staring at her now it became apparent that he'd be feeling sensation very soon, and she'd go the way of all those others girls before her.

Katie's breaths took longer between each intake. They'd became more laboured, more of a struggle. Her eyes remained tightly closed but tears still somehow found their way through the swelling and leaked onto her equally bruised cheeks. Her body was turning even paler, ghost-like. She tried to twist in her sleep bringing a snigger from Ditch as the chains prevented the movement once again. Never gets old that one. He could almost see Katie's mind telling her to give up, it was written across her pained battered face. Ditch had become an expert in such matters. He'd seen it all. Hell he'd caused it all.

Ditch unzipped his boiler suit as he watched the girl's

life slowly fading in front of him. He tugged at his cock as her breathing slowed further still. Ditch leant closer to her face, inches away, he could feel the lack of breath scarcely escaping her nose and mouth. The faint puffs barely produced anything. He slipped his hand on to her scarred chest and felt the pathetic attempts it made to rise. While there he slid his hand upwards to cop a quick feel of her breast, but that could wait till after she died. There were bigger things at stake. He moved his hand back down to her stomach wanting to feel the exact moment she passed with both his sight and touch. Katie wasn't long for this world.

He yanked his cock when he thought he'd witnessed her last breath, but then felt her abdomen agonisingly rise once more. Fucking tease. He released his dick and grabbed the nearby pliers eyeing up the fingers on her right hand. Her index finger was badly bruised from being snapped back and forth a couple of days back, it looked prime for removing. "Would be a kindness," he told her aloud, but Katie was in no condition to hear him.

Inflicting more damage to kill her wasn't his objective however. He wanted Katie to give in, to let herself die. That was the real thrill, the grand prize, the fucking jackpot. He'd already pushed his involvement in her final moments too far if he was completely honest with himself. The whiteness in her face and body was a clear indication that the bleeding out was causing her death, not the fragility of her mind. If he took a finger at this point he'd definitely witness her death, but he'd be the direct cause of it. Not her. Well he was always the cause of it, he guffawed, but never the guy to execute that killer blow, that was on them. Not that a jury would ever see it that way.

If he was being a hundred percent truthful to the process he really should have been cauterising her wound. No matter how much their bitching and whining led to him bringing the pain in the first place, he always patched them up afterwards. Haphazardly, barbarically even, mostly without any pain meds, but enough for the brutality not to be the direct cause of death. Even when he sawed an arm off, poked an eye out, or blowtorched their pussy, he always made sure they physically survived. Then he'd leave it to their distraught minds to deliver that awe-inspiring killer blow.

He stared at the bloody gap were her toe use to be once more. The bleeding seemed to have finally stopped, but that was only half the problem for Katie. Stuck in two minds Ditch watched her laboured breathing a little longer, it had slowed further still. She was at death's door, possibly even banging on it. Ditch tried to shake away any thoughts of her death being a cheat. His cellar, his leader board, his rules. Maybe the feeling wouldn't be as powerful as usual, but he was still as hard as a rock so clearly her death was doing something for him.

Ditch slid his hand back down his boiler suit. Began grabbing his dick tighter as he leaned into Katies face once more. He was so close that he licked the tears from her swollen eyes, but that was too much for him. He came instantly. Fuck. "Well, there's no point you dying now," he joked with a chuckle as he began to wipe the cum from his cock and boiler suit using the only clean part of the bloody rag barely covering Katie.

Katie made a last gasp for breath. Her head tilted slightly to the side and her eyes began to roll into the back of her head. It would have been the perfect moment for her to die, her opportunity to steal Ditch's win. He quite literally would have blown his wad early if she picked this moment to finally surrender, to succumb to his inhumane torment and unwavering torture. Ditch's black heart stopped for a beat. He was genuinely worried he would be cheated of the thrill he sought. She'd still given him a nice feeling, his sticky hands and cum-stained outfit were proof of that, but it wasn't the same.

…Then Katie took another breath.

Her eyes returned to the front of her head as her stomach began to rise with a little more vigour and regularity.

"Good girl," Ditch told her as he realised she'd decided to still live. Katie was going to survive the night, especially if he stitched up that wound which he knew he should be getting on with. Ditch grabbed his lighter and a needle and made his way to her foot.

"I'll make you fucking suffer tomorrow for teasing me like that," he told Katie before aiming the lit lighter at the gaping hole where her toe once was. Her screams were yet another indication that she was still alive.

Reaper

Katie was up to number six on the leader board with day seventeen scrawled alongside it. A recently developed Polaroid taken in her sleep was pinned beside the number. She looked an absolute state in the photo with her face battered and bruised beyond recognition and even more hair ripped out. It was all the new norm for Katie who hadn't been able to open her left eye for the last few days such was the extent of the swelling. Her tits were showing within the picture too which wasn't Ditch's usual framing as he often just concentrated on their beaten faces, but after the abuse he'd given them of late they felt like a worthy edition in their blackened state. Complimented her fucked up face nicely.

Despite her dazed condition, Katie noticed when she awoke from her latest blackout that Ditch had left the room. His empty stool rested in the middle of the cellar with a hunting knife stuck upright in the seat. Fresh blood had carelessly slid down the blade on to the chair forming a crimson pool of her blood. Despite the knife being unattended and within Katie's eyesight she had no hope of reaching it and her right eye fixed on another weapon equally out of reach as she stirred.

Resting against the leg of the tool table was a bloodstained heavy-duty pipe wrench. The very same wrench that was used to crack Ryan's skull open and turn his face into pulp. It was the first time Katie had seen the wrench since witnessing Ditch use it to cold-bloodedly murder her beloved. Another one of Ditch's sick games. He'd purposefully left it in plain sight to drive Katie further into insanity and closer to death, and it was working. A massive urge surged through her to just slit her wrists and be fucking done with it all, and she would have done exactly that had the knife been more accessible. Instead, she just stared heartbroken at the wrench that took Ryan's life and permanently ruined hers.

Her nose was broken again. Ditch had fucked it up during the night and then badly reset it. It was practically useless now. Just there for show, although not aesthetically pleasing in the slightest. It looked ugly and lumpy amidst the black and purple bruising that spread across the rest of her face. Completely out of shape despite the attempted reset as the bone was fragmented with no chance of being properly fixed. In skilled hands maybe some small part of it could have possibly been salvaged, but not in the hands of Ditch. His idea of fixing something was hitting it in the opposite direction it was pointing. Ditch was the furthest thing you could get from a doctor.

Behind Katie, the cloaked figure hidden in the shadows awkwardly shuffled as he tried to get a better view of her nose now that she was awake.

"You still here?" she asked him, without really asking him. It was more of a statement.

"Didn't think I would be," he replied acknowledging her for the first time in the seventeen days since her arrival in this small slice of hell. He angled himself forward slightly as Katie turned to look at the no longer mute bystander.

Some of his face and body had escaped the shadow. Katie saw for herself the thick black cloak that reached all the way to the bottom of his feet and stretched to his bony fingertips. Those bony fingers were wrapped around a scythe that he clutched tightly in his left hand. Katie hadn't noticed the scythe before despite it being around six feet long, much like its owner. The curved blade at the end was razor-sharp but a dull colour, the silver gleam a distant memory. The blade had caused too much bloodshed down the years and now edged more towards black than its previous silver. Not quite as black as the shadows or his cloak, but getting there.

The figure's face was stripped of its skin much like the rest of his body. It was just a skull now, albeit one with dark eyes that could quite literally peer into people's souls. He didn't appear to have pupils as such, just two little blacker than black marbles in his eye sockets. Katie needed no introduction to his rotten teeth, she'd seen them for the last two weeks. They looked no different out of the shadows than in. They remained disgusting and yellow and the only part of his body that wasn't black and white. If possible they looked a little more filthy slightly closer up, but that seemed to be the only discernible difference. Katie couldn't mistake the look now that he'd revealed more of himself from the shadows. However implausible, the figure had to be the Grim Reaper.

Reaper's dark eyes flicked from Katie to the knife sticking upright on the stool. "He use the knife again?"

Reaper asked with a tinge of regret in his surprisingly bland voice. Not regret towards the violent act however, regret that he missed it. He'd been away on important business. While he spent a lot of time in the cellar Katie noticed that he did disappear plenty too. She wasn't sure how or why, but could always feel when he returned. The feeling was like an ice-cold draft, enough to make her wonder whether there was a back door to the cellar despite how silly and desperate that sounded. This was not the sort of place that would have a fire exit.

Katie nodded towards her leg answering his question. Several fresh scars ran from her ankle to the top of her hip where Ditch had guided the knife repeatedly up and down her leg. Not deep enough to nick an artery, but with enough pressure to draw blood and leave yet more marks on her already fragile legs. Flakes of melted skin fell during the repeated cuts causing her legs to burn alongside the stings of the lacerations. She knew better than to show the pain when Ditch committed what he'd describe as 'trivial torture,' that just encouraged him to inflict more, so Katie took her lumps without letting a single whimper escape her mouth.

Reaper took note of her deformed foot as he surveyed her newly scarred leg. The missing toes were healing poorly he observed, especially the new stub. It had turned a nasty shade of purple that didn't look at all right. Reaper couldn't help but smile. "You know he practically considers himself an artist," he stated, once again sounding not in the least bit appalled by Ditch's actions. If anything, he sounded like a fanboy.

"And how do you see him?" Katie mumbled catching the enthusiasm he hadn't hidden well. She had plenty of other things she'd have loved to have said to the macabre observer but for the moment she decided to go along with the conversation. This was the first time she'd spoken to anyone other than Ditch in over two weeks and while the Grim Reaper wouldn't be her first choice for some chit-chat, he was her only choice.

"As interesting," Reaper mused while moving himself even closer to Katie. "You know I once missed an appointment while watching him use a branding iron on a young girls face." Reaper's attention shifted to the leader board across the room. He scanned the board settling somewhere near the bottom. "That's the girl," he told Katie pointing to a mutilated redhead who looked like a Batman villain with half her face burnt to a crisp.

Katie didn't turn to the board to see who Reaper meant, and wouldn't be able to see the picture from her position anyway with one eye closed and the other barely open. Not that she wanted to see. All the girls represented to Katie was what she had coming so the less she saw the better. It wasn't a lack of respect or not wanting to know the other victims, it was self-preservation. Ditch often used the previous girls to coerce an emotional response from Katie but once she realised he was succeeding she closed herself off from them. Hopefully, they lived in other people's memories, but they couldn't be part of hers. The weight of pain they brought with them was too much to bare. Reaper sensed her disinterest in the picture but carried on his story regardless.

"Death was pissed I missed the appointment. This guy had jumped out of a twenty-storey building. I was meant to be there, but I couldn't take my eyes off Ditch's handiwork." Reaper stated while lapsing into a daydream as he remembered the sick use of the branding iron on the poor helpless girl. He remembered the screams and look of shock as she smelt her own cheek burning beside her nose before that too melted, it literally slid off her face, or at least that's how Reaper remembered it.

He let the image linger in his mind for a moment longer before returning to his story. "The guy survived with just a couple of broken legs. Thought it was a miracle, so he changed his tune. Thanked God for his second chance at life." Reaper regaled. "Really the lucky bastard should have thanked Ditch." He reflected. "Funny how these things work."

"You're as sick as him," Katie told Reaper through gritted teeth. She'd waited all this time to hear what he had to say for himself and hadn't liked a single word of it. It had been quite the revelation that he was an agent of Death, but at the same time Katie had suspected. He had that aura about him from the beginning. She felt surrounded by the stench of death both in a metaphorical and literal sense from the moment she was tossed through the door into the unmerciful cellar. Reaper confirming her suspicions hadn't changed a thing, apart from the fact that she now had two assholes recounting stories of innocent dead girls.

"Hey," Reaper replied taken back by her insight. "I couldn't do what he does," he added rather defensively. "I was a business major, not a fucking psycho!." Reaper stood from his seat and marched out of the shadows. Katie wasn't aware he could do that. She also wasn't aware she could hurt his feelings, but no fucks were given. He'd sat back for weeks watching her get tortured, raped, and systematically destroyed, so his feelings were the least of her concerns.

The light in the cellar dimmed as the shadows caught up with Reaper who had regained his composure. "Like I said, he's just interesting," he told Katie in a tone that was slightly more apologetic than previously, but one hundred percent insincere. "I turn up for the appointment, but the woman doesn't die on time. She holds on that little bit longer, sometimes a lot longer." He pointed at Katie. "You should know." Reaper leant towards the knife wanting to reach out and touch the bloody blade. He resisted the urge. "It's the not knowing. The waiting." He added. "In my line of work that's exciting. Unpredictable. Rare."

"Can you save me?" Katie asked on the verge of tears and thoroughly done with the small talk. The pain from the fresh cuts along with the chance to actually talk to someone, or something, had overwhelmed her. Her emotions began to rise and it didn't help that the bloody pipe wrench was constantly in view as well, taunting her just like Ditch had planned. The images of Ryan being destroyed by the weapon flicked into Katie's head but she shook them away, along with some of the forming tears. She wanted to cry. To break. To fucking snap and disappear into the comfort hysteria might offer. But not for the first time these last few weeks she stopped herself. For some ungodly reason, she had to survive.

"Only when you stop the waiting. Only when you embrace death," Reaper answered like some kind of doomed prophet.

"You think dying is saving myself?" Katie answered with a wave of underlining anger in her voice but also a resentful element of awareness that Reaper was telling her the truth. It wasn't what she wanted to hear, but that didn't make it any less factual. Reaper sensed her mixed feelings so continued his sales pitch sounding more like a used car salesman than a prophet now.

"If you saw yourself in a mirror, you'd agree."

He drifted towards the leader board examining the different pictures on display. Each one looked uglier than the last. Faces half burnt off. Eyes missing. Cheeks ripped apart and ears torn. Teeth missing in shredded mouths. Jaws dislocated to almost comical proportions, or by the looks of the girl fourth from top completely fucking missing. And these were just their faces. Luckily most of the pictures tended not to show the rest of their abused and devastated bodies but Reaper had seen the full results and even the photos on the board didn't do the barbarism justice.

Ditch really had broken and disfigured these girls beyond all recognition. He'd taken their wills and every drop of hope and happiness they ever had. He was an evil brutal man who took joy in bringing these girls to the very edge of death and then forced them to take the leap into its open arms like it was their choice. Into Reaper's open arms. Death had become a salvation for all these tortured souls. Reaper really did admire Ditch's work, he'd never seen anyone else quite like him.

Reaper looked down at Katie from his position beside the board. If his eyes could convey emotion there may have been a tinge of sorrow in them, a very small tinge, but as he mentioned he wasn't as sadistic as Ditch. More the messenger than the message itself.

"I've been watching him for the last four years. No one escapes. Every girl dies," he stated as a cold hard fact that was unequivocally true. He took a knowing glance at the deep dark stain on the cellar floor that could never be removed. "It's just a matter of giving up hope. You can't escape, but you can win. Simply don't let him see you die. Rob him of his pleasure," Reaper suggested believing it really was the best possible outcome. After letting that thought sit for a moment he piped up from his serious tone. "That way I can get on with my day at least, until the next girl."

Now Katie really did want to burst into tears. She wanted to shout, and scream, and cry until she died of dehydration knowing what the sick twisted Reaper had told her was the undeniable truth. She hated him more than ever for stating the facts in such a stony manner. There was no remorse in his dead eyes, although she guessed there probably couldn't have been. But surely he could do something? Anything? He had to be able to help her in a way that didn't involve her simply dying at the hands of this demented fucking cunt.

"You could undo my straps?" Katie stated, trying her best to put on a brave face and not melt into a pool of despair.

His eyes once again returned to the grisly unremovable stain on the cellar floor. "You don't want that."

It was too late anyway as the pair heard the thick brown cellar door begin to unbolt.

New Outfit

The heavy brown door swung open as Ditch entered with a shit-eating grin spread across his face and a clear plastic bag grasped in his hand. Inside the bag was a yellow cheerleaders' outfit that even within its wrapping appeared noticeably too small for Katie. The outfit was in two parts, a tight crop top, and a tiny mini skirt. The sort of skirt Katie's dad would have described as a belt in her younger more rebellious years and promptly ask her to change into something more appropriate.

"You're going to look great in this," Ditch announced as he breezed past Reaper paying him no attention whatsoever. Reaper took a sneak peek in the bag as Ditch approached Katie and nodded his approval. She really would look great in it, he thought as he slid back into the shadows behind the bed to watch the show.

Ditch stopped just short of Katie displaying his overly beaming fake smile. For someone who always had such putrid breath, his teeth were remarkably white Katie subconsciously observed. A stark contrast to the Grim Reaper who'd now settled in his normal place behind her. Ditch was genuinely excited to see her in the outfit, but he was more trying to antagonise her further with the ridiculous cartoony smile. Katie knew the drill by now. Everything was a spiteful game to him, a chance to humiliate her more with the end game being to completely break her.

He took the outfit from the bag confirming that it really

was far too short for her, but that was the intention. "I think it's for a thirteen-year-old, but you'll squeeze into it nicely for me right?" He asked, although it wasn't really a question, she had no choice. However her recent conversation with Reaper had given Katie the impression that maybe she did have a choice, it wasn't one she particularly liked, but it had to be better than being this asshole's plaything. She could always say no and die.

Katie shook her head much to Ditch's bemusement. He loved it when they acted all tough. Normally this kind of defiance happened at the beginning before they truly understood the nightmare they were stuck in, but every now and then he'd get some resistance weeks in and they were always fun days. He wandered to his tool (weapons) table and picked up a pair of brass knuckles. They looked big and chunky rather than something discreet. These weren't made for self-defence or anything subtle, these were made to make you shit your pants the moment you saw them. Ditch looked back to Katie who carried on shaking her head, "Correct answer," he told her as his stupid smile morphed into a more sinister smirk that suited his evil face more.

The first punch was directed at Katie's scarred midriff. The impact felt like he'd put his hand right through her, and she wished he had. She could almost feel him fucking with her innards such was the force. But he hadn't punched a hole through her now skinny frame, just driven all the wind out of her frail body and broken a rib or two. Katie couldn't breathe. She twisted and turned, gasping for air like a fish out of water all while Ditch smirked and Reaper intently observed wondering what was next. If he could have watched with a bag of popcorn in hand, he would have.

Reaper did continue to encourage Katie though. He told her to embrace the feeling surging through her body, not fight it. Not to go searching for that breath she needed to continue. That he could take her away from all this suffering if she just welcomed the pain this time around and let it become too much for her. He was cheering for her death, and inwardly, so was Katie. She wanted this to be the end. The cheerleader outfit probably wasn't the hill to die on, he'd done a hell of a lot worse, but she knew the suffering would be never-ending. So why not take a stand now? Why not just fucking die? Be done with it.

But her body and mind didn't work like that. Her body continued to gasp for air, for life, while her mind tried to cope with the pain rather than let it swamp her. Both body and mind continued to be in defence mode defying her will under the pretence of protecting her. The moment Katie got her breathing under some sort of control Ditch ripped her skimpy top off and punched her hard in her exposed and already extremely badly bruised tits. The sick fucker didn't just punch one of them with the brass knuckles, he made sure to double jab and connect with both.

Unlike the previous punch that prevented her shouting out, this time Katie screamed in agony. Music to Ditch's ears. New bruises already somehow found room to form on her defaced breasts. Ditch reached down and squeezed the left one hard with the brass knuckle still in hand, and it felt like it was going to pop such was the unrelenting pressure. If Ditch could have torn the tit clean from her body in that moment he would have, he certainly fucking tired. He had succeeded in doing it once before to a girl long before the concept of the leader board came along, but admittedly he'd already cut most of it off beforehand. Yanking it clear with his bare hands had been the finishing touch.

"You going to put it on for me now?" Ditch asked. Again it didn't sound like a question, despite being phrased as such. He took the tiny top and laid it over Katie's bare body like he was trying to gauge whether it would fit right. For him it definitely fitted right. For Katie, it would be a tight squeeze despite her emaciated body. "Is about time you wore something new, you filthy cunt. Really have let yourself go," he laughed. Katie tried her best to spit on the top, or Ditch, but ended up just dribbling on her chin. That evoked more laughter from Ditch who was enjoying every second of her renewed insolence. He slid the brass knuckles off and retreated back to the weapons table.

He picked up a blow torch and looked in Katie's direction. The fear in her eyes alone was enough for that weapon to have already done its job, maybe another time. The claw hammer was always a favourite, but he'd used that on her already during the first few days. He briefly considered the heavy wrench that killed her boyfriend but thought he'd save that one for a special occasion. Not that this wasn't a special occasion - every day Ditch got to torture some poor innocent girl was a special occasion to him, but he'd save the wrench for a milestone. Assuming she'd reach another one of course.

Ditch settled on the nail gun as he hadn't used it since eight girls back. He'd got a bit carried away that time and fully pinned the girl to the bed using the little skin she had left on her bony arms and legs. She only lasted two days in total and sat practically bottom of the leader board. In her defence, it had been a pretty rough start to her stay, Ditch reasoned. He'd promised himself to be a little more careful in the future. He wanted them near death and to then take the final step themselves, which in theory she did, but this girl mostly died because he went full savage straight away. He got no real joy out of that one, other than the obvious pleasure he got from torturing the cunt. But no ultimate buzz.

Still, a couple of nails wouldn't kill this bitch. Katie had endured a lot more and this wasn't her first day. The two-day girl had pissed, shitted, and puked, all at the same time when that first nail shot through her body, Katie was made of sterner stuff. Ditch strolled towards her playfully twirling the nail gun in his hand like it was a toy. "You changed your mind?"

"Just kill me," Katie mumbled as she struggled with the increased pain surging through her body. Her ribs were definitely broken.

"Death is your choice, not mine." Ditch preached like

the rehearsed speech it was. He'd told his victims this so many times that it came across as perfunctory despite his excitement at the prospect. "I can facilitate, but you have to take that final step yourself," he told her, licking his lips with his hand already rubbing his stiffening cock through his boiler suit. The very thought of Katie giving in at his hands induced some pre-cum.

Katie contemplated what he had to say while trying to ignore the way he lustfully leered at her. Dying at his hands now would give him that buzz he wanted, Reaper had made that clear, and Ditch wasn't being subtle about the fact either. Reaper had suggested as a counterpoint dying when he wasn't around, that she'd win that way, but it didn't feel like a win. It didn't really feel possible either. Clearly if her body was just going to tap out it would have done so already.

However she died Ditch would get something out of it, and she'd be dead. But death could bring peace, she hoped. Although the idea that Reaper was waiting for her on the other side didn't exactly fill her with the hope that death would be a fulfilling release. Reaper watched on, encouraging Katie to die as the pain continued to sweep through her body. It felt like he was telling her to get it over with one way or another. His previous suggestion of dying when Ditch wasn't around had been replaced with just dying by any means possible. Would she just be swapping one evil psychotic asshole's wishes for another? Whatever happened. they'd both win, and she'd lose. But like Reaper told her, if she could see herself now she would welcome death.

Katie took too long to reply so Ditch fired a nail straight through the top of her right thigh. He quickly followed it with a second and third shot as once again he got carried away with the nail gun. He couldn't help it, he fucking loved it. She screamed out in anguish as the nail easily punched through her raw skin. The nails weren't quite long enough to go right through her leg and pin her to the bed, but that was of little consolation. The suffering was once again unbearable, except somehow she did continue to bear it. Katie remained in a constant state of near-death, just as Ditch had promised, and just as Reaper had warned. Ditch licked the fresh blood pouring from her leg to add insult to injury while Katie continued to despise her crap options.

He took the cheerleader top off her prone body and settled it on the nearby stool next to the knife he briefly considered using but decided against. He was having too much fun with the nail gun. Ditch studied her ruined body wondering what to hurt next. He was really in the mood now to cause damage the likes of which she had never felt before. Katie was missing a couple of toes already and her legs were all burnt and cut up. Practically fucking melted. Now she had three nails stuck to the top of them as well, along with all the other sadistic shit he'd put her through. What more could he do?

Ditch considered firing a nail into her pussy but he had other plans for that. Her tummy was scared and her tits looked a right fucking state. They barely turned him on anymore looking like chiselled coal from all the abuse. He could cut a nipple off though? His cruel eyes settled on her face instead. Through the swelling, she stared back at him with utter contempt and irrefutable fear. A delightful mixture. The idea of nail gunning one of her eyes made Ditch feel all warm and fuzzy inside, but that would probably kill her. He could possibly start with that on the next girl when it's early enough for her to take it, he compromised. Then remembered the all too quick death of the two-day girl. It was hard to strike the right balance at times.

Ditch reached down and took Katie's head moving the nail gun close to her left eye. He teased the action with his finger wavering over the trigger. She tried to plead with him but the words wouldn't form and he wouldn't listen anyway, she knew that. But maybe she should welcome the shot? Katie had no doubt in her mind that no matter how hard her body was fighting it couldn't withstand a nail to the eye, maybe this would be the release she desired.

He tilted Katie's head so that her eye was out the firing line, but instead her ear was in prime position as he fired the nail gun. The sickening thud of the nail piercing her ear and sticking into the bed rang through Katie's head. Blood and cartilage spilled as a metallic sound invested the little that remained of hearing. She didn't dare move not knowing whether the nail had stuck into the bed or not, as one slight movement would rip her fucking ear off. If any of it remained.

It wasn't the same as the eye he wanted to take, but it

was a fair middle ground. She looked ridiculous stuck to the bed by her ear so Ditch settled for amusement rather than the excitement he'd have felt with the eye. Plus this shot hadn't killed her, just brought her another step closer to death both in pain and humiliation. Can't be too many people in this world who have been nail gunned to a bed by their ear. That had to sting whatever was left of her feeble pride.

Ditch left her like that while he retrieved the cheerleader outfit. For the shortest of moments, she became the most free she'd been in weeks when he removed both the chains holding her legs in place, but she couldn't take advantage. Her ear was pinned to the bed. The large nail had penetrated both the flesh and threadbare mattress and stuck to the reinforced wood underneath the bed. Ditch hadn't known if it would work and had been pleasantly surprised to find it did - learn something new every day. He'd definitely be using that trick on the next worthless slut he dragged to the cellar.

The teeny yellow cheerleader skirt slowly slid up Katie's body as Ditch took his time. His fingers scraped along her burning legs as they went. Each unwelcome touch felt like it set ablaze her flaky melted raw skin and further stung the recent knife wounds. He stretched the skirt over her anorexic hips and grabbed her gaunt ass. She really was wasting away. Good thing he liked them skinny, Ditch deliberated. With the skirt in place, he reapplied the chains with a little extra tightness thrown in for good measure. The little glimpse of freedom was nothing but an illusion, but Katie was already aware of that. She harboured no plans of escape at this point. Her last hope had been Reaper, and he wasn't going to do shit.

"How do you want the nail to come out?" Ditch asked as a genuine question. That was the thing he actually gave her a choice over? "I could yank it out? Use the claw hammer? Cut the ear off? Let it come out naturally?" He laughed at the last one. "Either way it needs to come out so I can get your new top on."

Katie didn't have an answer, just tears. A few days back she wondered if she could even cry anymore, turned out however dehydrated her body was it could still produce an abundance of fresh tears when nailed to a fucking bed by the ear and having some creep run his dirty fingers up her pealing diced up useless legs.

"I'll make the choice," Ditch informed her like it was his good deed for the day. He grabbed the claw hammer from the table. It always came back to the claw hammer he thought fondly. It took him several attempts but he finally pulled the nail from Katie's ear. It was stuck in there good. She'd once again passed out from the pain, a regular habit of hers now. Fucking pussy. It made it easier for Ditch to unchain her arms and slide the scant cheerleader's top on, not that she was ever really a problem. She could be awake with twenty coffees and half a dozen energy drinks in her and he'd still be able to handle the bitch just fine.

Ditch looked down admiring his handiwork. She'd already managed to get blood on the top courtesy of her ear but he'd punish her for that later. She really did look stupidly fucking hot in the undersized outfit, Ditch thought despite her decimated condition. At this point her face was starting to resemble a chewed-up rubber. He'd never brought back anyone as young as the outfit was intended for but for the first time, he was tempted. For the moment he'd enjoy Katie though as Ditch was all about living in the present and Katie didn't have long to live by his reckoning.

He stripped from his boiler suit with his dick already hard as granite and climbed on top of Katie while she remained passed out. He rammed his cock inside her bone-dry pussy but she didn't awake. Ditch chuckled to himself as he considered the number of vile ways he could wake the ungrateful bitch halfway though. Top of the list was nibbling on what was left of her ear.

The Kidnapping

When Katie regained consciousness Ditch stood over her. The heavy-duty pipe wrench that had moments earlier taken Ryan away from her forever hung loosely in his hand as Ryan's blood dripped on to Katie's face and hair while she looked up at their attacker. The screws and bolts on the massive wrench had indistinguishable chunks of flesh stuck to them and Katie briefly thought she saw one of Ryan's eyes but looked away before confirming it.

It all felt like a dream, but that was partly down to the daze she was in after being inadvertently head-butted by Ryan and very purposefully cracked in the jaw by Ditch. Smacking against the car after the punch completed the trifecta of headshots that currently made her eyes blurry and her mind hazy. But it wasn't a dream. The blood and chucks glued to the wrench looked and smelt too real for it to be a dream. Ryan really was dead, and his killer really was menacingly standing over her.

Katie screamed and Ditch let her. They were in the middle of nowhere and the odds of a passer-by or some farmhand hearing her were remote at this time of night. Plus what the fuck were they going to do? Ditch had a big bloody wrench in hand, and if need be, a gun in his pick-up. If someone wanted to be a hero, let them. But there were no heroes around, only a villain.

Ditch leant down beside Katie positioning himself to allow the running blood from the wrench to continue to spill on to her terrified face. She tried to pull her head aside but Ditch grabbed her cheeks and mouth with his other hand and squeezed them holding her still in a vice-like grip. He didn't look like he should have that sort of strength, but he did. He spat in Katie's face for good measure when she tried to further resist shaking her head side to side. The weak resistance quickly gave way to more tears and resignation as his spit ran down her nose getting lost in Ryan's blood while Ditch kept his hand clawed tightly around her face.

"Don't worry," he announced with a beaming smile on his face. "I'm not going to kill you." He said it like he meant it too, but there was a caveat. That being he was going to torture her beyond all reason to the point that not only would she welcome death, but she'd be the one to take the final step towards it. She didn't know that was the condition in that moment but Ditch was already excited for her future. He let go of Katie's cheek freeing her from his grasp and she instantly tried to crawl away. They always tried to crawl away Ditch mused, watching Katie on her hands and knees.

It wasn't as if Katie believed she could crawl to freedom, it was just instinct. That part of your brain that knows you have to get away whether there's a possibility of it or not. It's all part of what Ditch was attempting to break within each of his victims, that glimmer of hope. The idea that somehow their life can go on while they should already know they're doomed. The human spirit is how he always described it when he articulated what exactly he was trying to crush. It was early on in Katie's journey so it was only natural she still had it - fuck! he'd be so disappointed if she didn't. It would have been a waste of everyone's time if she didn't even make it off the starting line.

"I'd been having such a shitty day," he told Katie like they were old friends. "You know those days where everything that could go wrong does," he smirked taking a moment to acknowledge her current predicament. "Well you know," he added trying to purposefully emphasise the irony of his statement and get a rise from her. Katie continued her painstakingly slow crawl trying to block out the sound of his cunty voice. There was nothing particularly awful sounding about his actual voice, but after what he'd done to Ryan every word sounded like nails to a chalkboard.

"Then I saw you and my day picked up instantly.' He snapped his fingers. "Just like that, all the bullshit earlier was forgotten." He let her crawl a little bit further watching her ass. She'd made about ten metres so he stepped aside and quietened down so it looked like he was out of sight as she chanced a look back. It was just the beginning of Ditch's mind games. He circled around the old Pontiac and began to casually walk alongside Katie as she crawled. She did her best not to look up at him but his presence was all too obvious. So was that fucking dripping blood from the wrench, had he re-dipped it or something?

Ditch stopped recounting the story of his crappy day and started to explain instead what he was going to do to her. How he was going to take her back to his cellar and have his way with her and torture her until she couldn't bear it anymore. He didn't spare any of the gory details either as he promised her that she would hate every single second of it and be begging for a death he won't grant her. His tone the whole time was factual, but with glee. He had done this many times over and the excitement hadn't depreciated. There was no diminishing returns here, every captured girl was a new intoxicating experience.

He'd let her crawl far enough. While he fancied his chances against any passer-by there was no need to invite trouble for the sake of it. He'd got this far through being careful when kidnapping his victims, always making sure they were alone, or easy to snatch. Preferably in a place where no one would stumble across his misadventures. Then he'd pack them into his pick-up and take them to his remote cabin. No fucking way was that ever being found, and even if it was, the chances of them finding the soundproof cellar seemed even more remote. Basically once he got them home that was it for them.

Already he'd broken his own kidnapping rules. He'd come across Katie after an earlier attempt to seize a different girl had fallen apart. She'd been with several other people when she should have been alone and then of all things, had ended up at the fucking airport. Not only could Ditch not get hold of her when planned, but now the bitch had left the country. Dumb fucking luck. So when he saw Katie sitting on the roof in the glow of the moonlight looking beautiful and ripe he had to have her despite the presence of the oaf boyfriend. He took a big chance deviating from his usual routine but seeing her now he knew he'd made the right decision.

Katie's head had cleared slightly from the punch and fall. The loss of Ryan would leave it in a partial haze forever, but she couldn't worry about that now. She'd crawled far enough to regain some strength and would only have one chance to get away from this fucking psycho. Considering she was in the middle of nowhere, she had no idea which way to go, but that was a problem for later. At the moment, her only concern was jumping to her feet and sprinting like crazy until she had nothing left.

"You're thinking of running aren't you?" Ditch laughed. Again, he loved this part. Everyone's reaction was all too similar. They had barely any choices, but still, it amused him greatly how they all followed the same path like they were the first to ever think it up. "I'll tell you what," he started looking down at Katie's bloody face with the added irony that it wasn't even her blood for once. Ditch had taken a massive sick pleasure in drowning the poor girl in her boyfriend's blood, a first for him so he was grateful for the new experience. It gave him a soft spot for her. Not a soft spot like he was going to let her go, more like he was going to enjoy her even more.

"I'll give you a ten-second head start. But… if I catch you it won't be pleasant." He told her while twisting the wrench in his hand. "Or… you don't run and I'll take it easy on you for the first day." Katie didn't need time to contemplate, she was on her feet ready to run while he was still talking but Ditch had no intent on letting her run whatever option she took. The moment she climbed to her feet he drove the massive pipe wrench into the back of her legs. Katie dropped to the ground only just managing to get her arms out in front of her to avoid another blow to the head.

Ditch began to count despite Katie being in no condition to run. It felt like her legs were broken such was the impact of the strike. Fortunately, they weren't but either way she couldn't stand let alone sprint into the darkness away from the nutcase. She tried to get to her feet again but it was no use, the pain was too much and instead she cried uncontrollably. Her head felt even worse and she just wanted to pass out or die with the brutal death of Ryan replaying on loop in her mind. No way Ditch would allow the latter though, not this early. When he reached the count of ten, Ditch grabbed Katie by the hair and dragged her towards the pick-up after delivering a very excitable "caught you," like they'd been playing chase. There was no chase however, Kate hadn't made it one step further than when he started counting.

Her hurting, but not broken legs scraped across the thin layer of stones while her scalp felt tight with every strand of hair being yanked. She tried swatting one of his hands away but that just resulted in Ditch stopping for a moment and punting her in the stomach several times. While she tried to recover control of her breathing he threw her shoes away and stared at her short grey skirt that was riding upwards and revealing her white knickers. If he hadn't wasted so much time already he'd have fucked her there and then. He'd been thinking about it ever since seeing her on the car roof kissing her boyfriend and fondling his dick. Despite the cover of nightfall he decided it was best not to take the chance despite his raging hard-on. There would be plenty of time for that later.

Reaching the pick-up Ditch poked his hand inside and retrieved a medical bag sitting on the front seat. From inside the bag he pulled out a syringe and plunged it into Katie's arm without a second thought. She hadn't even realised what he'd done. She just felt a slight sting and carried on momentary struggling to get away before her eyes began to fade. It could have been the traumatic events of the last twenty minutes that finally sent her into a long spout of unconsciousness, but it wasn't. Ditch had drugged her.

Ditch tossed the pipe wrench into the bay of the pick-up before stuffing Katie into the passenger seat. He wrapped a chain around her neck keeping her upright in the seat and slid on her seatbelt. He would have made some kind of safety joke to her but she was already out cold. She wouldn't wake up for the journey but Ditch took no chances locking the glove box in front of her that contained his hand-gun. He had a routine for this situation and never deviated, making sure that no slip-ups would occur, and his track record had so far been flawless.

He took one last look around the beautiful surroundings. A little of the beauty had admittedly been lost with the blood on the floor and the whole area looking like a murder rape scene, but even someone as sadistic and

fucked up as Ditch could appreciate a lovely view.
Especially when he'd mostly be spending the next
however long in a cellar. It could be just a few days in the
dank underground room, but he reckoned this one would
last longer. There was something about her.

Taking one last walk to the blood-stained Pontiac Fiero
Ditch reached inside and retrieved Katie's bag hoping it
would contain a few bits he could keep as a trophy after
her death. While there he grabbed a couple more bloody
rolls and some cake from the bonnet. After all, he had a
long drive ahead of him.

Might Die

Katie's breathing had almost come to a stop, such was the gap between breaths. Sweat dripped from her forehead and face, the feverish type rather than the overheating kind. The fever could have existed for any number of reasons given the current wrecked shape of her body. For starters, Katie's swollen eyes had doubled in size, or at least one of them had, the other was gone. A day earlier Ditch had decided it was about time she lost an eye, and he had made a big announcement of it like it was exciting news. He then instantly want to work excavating it with the end of a crowbar. Afterwards, he'd stuck her eye to one of the screws near the top of the wrench in the same way as one of Ryan's had stuck there after Ditch demolished him. It stared at her all day long like some kind of way too realistic googly eye, yet another way to torment her.

The pain from the ripped out eye had been relentless. Several times her body had gone into shock and Ditch eagerly watched on believing this was the moment she'd give in. Give in, like it was her choice! He'd prised her fucking eye out with a crowbar. Katie hadn't even believed that was possible until it happened to her. She hadn't said a word since which Ditch duly punished her for believing she was giving him the silent treatment. But her brain had finally snapped. She couldn't even form the hate filled words to screech at him anymore, she was done.

The fever could have also been caused by the flap of cheek hanging from her face. Ditch had taken a cheese grater to that courtesy of the silent treatment. It hadn't made her talk, quite the opposite in fact, as she once again passed out from the pain. Katie had lost track of how many times she'd passed out and drifted between consciousness in the last couple of weeks. Before the day he kidnapped her she was certain she'd never blacked out once before in her entire life. Now it was a daily occurrence.

Other than her wrenched out eyeball and diced-up cheek the third big candidate for her fever was her feet and legs which had started turning a vile green colour over the last day or two. It was probably inevitable the infection from her missing toes would get worse, but the peeled legs had become infected too. She started to look and smell like a fucking zombie. Ditch had fed her mouthfuls of antibiotics but they hadn't helped. She was way beyond Ditch's *webMD* impersonations and over-the-counter meds. Katie needed a full medical team and fast, but Ditch had no intention of supplying one. If she wanted to be free of all the agony and pain caused by her harrowing catalogue of injuries and problems then all she had to do was simply fucking die.

Her new undersized cheerleader outfit had lasted less than a day looking crisp. In the three days since he'd forced the uniform on her, it had become stained beyond all recognition. There was simply no way you could have known it started out yellow as the outfit was now a horrible reddish-brown colour after pints of blood had been spilled. The blood had mixed with plenty of Katie's vomit, and piss stains had soiled the skirt, both hers and

Ditch's. He'd chucked a couple of buckets of water over Katie to clean the outfit but all that had succeeded in doing was give her a cold, which incidentally was at the very bottom of her list of concerns.

She'd been trapped in this hell hole for twenty days now and stood fifth on the leader board, joint with three other unfortunate souls. A quick glance at the board would tell you that barring the infamous day five this was the most popular day for the girls to die. Day five Ditch had summarised was the day when the girls with no actual character or strength couldn't handle it anymore and gave in before the real pain began. They were the insufferable daddy's-girl-types who hadn't worked a day in their life and couldn't handle a fucking paper cut let alone being blowtorched and raped. Pathetic.

Day twenty on the other hand, was when the more resilient girls who had endured and endured and endured and then finally realised that all there was to come was more. They'd held on admirably and given Ditch great pleasure before something snapped inside them. He'd seen it in Katie when he clawed her eye out and her silences afterwards confirmed it. He'd finally broken her. But girls like her didn't die immediately after being defeated. The brain had to accept the fact that it was broken first, and the mind had to realise that all hope was now forever lost, then it would be time. Ditch reckoned he'd almost subconsciously taken the eye a few days before day twenty to back up his own theory.

Reaper knew day twenty was going to be the day too.

Like Ditch, he was aware day twenty was the one when several of the tougher girls finally perished. He had been wracking his brain to think of a name for the day to mark the occasion but hadn't come up with anything solid yet. He wanted to ask Katie for suggestions but she hadn't looked or spoken to him since the whole eye incident, clearly holding him accountable too. Reaper always found this unfair but as several of the other girls had acted the same way he had to conclude that it was him, not them. Still, he was just doing his job. It wasn't as though he'd ever physically hurt any of them himself.

He'd given up encouraging Katie to let herself drift towards death, he didn't feel he needed to anymore considering how in disrepair she was. Plus she hadn't listened to him anyway. If Katie had taken his advice she would have died before the crow-barred eye, cheese grated cheek, and the whole looking like losing a leg to gangrene thing. He could have saved her a whole world of extra suffering, but she'd refused to die and had turned down his advice. It was commendable but stupid, Reaper thought. They all die in the end. There is no escaping this place, or Reaper for that matter, but she had stubbornly hung on like some kind of fucking martyr.

She wasn't the first to rebuff Reaper's advice, plenty of the other girls had too. The stronger ones all still believed there was some way out of this mess that involved them being alive, if not in one piece. Pure stubbornness. Pig-headedness. If only they'd seen the horrors he had witnessed in the cruel unforgiving cellar. He'd tried to explain to them that every victim's stay here ended the same way, but again they all believed they were different. None of them were different, not a single one. They all choose the extreme cruelty and barbarism of Ditch and the cellar over the freedom he was offering… right up until they didn't. In the end, they all embraced his exit strategy but not before putting themselves through extra misery and ghastly torture first. He wondered if they had listened to him straight away whether he'd be seen more as a saviour than the accomplice they all accused him of being.

Despite Katie's struggle for breaths, she was aware Ditch was leering over her with his hand once again tightly around his cock waiting for her to die. She could feel his rancid breath on what remained of her face. Could hear the excitement ticking away inside him at, least in her mind she could hear it. Katie's ear hadn't recovered from the nail gun blast, like it had any chance of, so he diced off the remains after he took her eye. Her ear had offered less resistance than the eye as Ditch cut through it with his knife leaving her overall hearing severely compromised with just the one ear remaining. Clearly hearing it or not she still knew what a ball of excitement Ditch was when she was knocking on deaths door, this wasn't her first rodeo.

Ditch had been relentless since she arrived, just as he'd promised. Not a single day had gone by without him torturing her. From losing a toe and her toe nails in the first few day to all the cuts, melting, slicing and dicing since. He'd been a fucking animal. He'd burnt and bruised her.

Ripped out her eye and chopped off her ear. Taunted her and spat abuse constantly while playing his little mind games like leaving the bloody pipe wrench in plain view or nailing her quite literally to the fucking bed. He regaled stories of all the past woman he'd butchered and read articles aloud about her disappearance and the investigation to find her. Mocked and mimicked how worried her parents were while they appealed to have their little girl safely returned to them.

Add into that all the times he'd viciously jammed his fingers down her mouth, up her ass, or into her cunt. How he'd held them tightly around her neck until she'd turned purple and was about to die only to release his grip at the very last moment and point and laugh as she struggled for breath. He hadn't stopped. He'd brought her close to death every day since she'd been here, so much so that the fucker was sitting alongside her waiting for her to take the leap. Every step of the way Ditch had committed these unforgivable acts with a smile on his face and a spring in his step. He was the Devil, of that she had no doubts. And if he wasn't the Devil, then he was something much worse.

But still she hadn't given in and just fucking died.

Why? She had nothing left. Ryan was dead. Her body was destroyed. Her parents wouldn't be able to handle seeing their 'little girl' in this deformed state. Sure they'd still love her and do everything they could for her, but seeing her like this would be too much for them to bear.

She didn't want to put them through that. Her soul felt forever tainted. Even if the impossible happened and she escaped this place what would life be? Could she even function beyond that cellar door anymore? She was blind in one eye and deaf in one ear. Her face looked chewed up and spat out. She wouldn't be surprised if her tits had to be cut off, or just simply fell off, along with her fucking disgusting infected legs and feet. She'd have nothing and be nothing.

Yet still she took a breath.

Katie had to think it wasn't life driving her anymore. She couldn't picture ever being in a relationship, having friends, or enjoying herself again. Living life was out of the question, she must still be breathing for another reason. That reason was licking his lips above her mutilated disfigured face with his hand currently wrapped around his erect veiny penis waiting to cum at the very moment of her death. She held on to life not only to deny him the satisfaction he so desperately craved from her death but to end his fucking life as well. How she would do that she didn't know. But in a cellar stuffed full of weapons the only thing that kept her fighting for every breath was that an opportunity would somehow present itself. It had to.

She defiantly took several more deeper breaths as her breathing steadied once again and it became clear she would survive another night. Ditch shook his head perplexed that she was going to make it through another day. Maybe he had underestimated her. He released his grip around his dick and disappointedly zipped back up. "Bitch," he literally spat at her. But the moment of frustration and annoyance didn't last long as he knew another day of torturing and abusing the poor resolute girl lay ahead.

He strolled to the leader board looking at a clock sitting on the weapons table and noting it had passed midnight. She really had survived another day. He moved her name tag and picture ahead of the girls that had jointly shared day twenty with Katie, scribbling day twenty-one beside her name instead. Katie was now second on the board with only one girl ahead of her. She really could make it he thought.

Although she'd have to survive tomorrow first.

Unwanted Gift

Ditch pinned a new Polaroid of Katie wearing a skimpy French maids outfit on to the leader board. The number beside it read day twenty-four and her name was positioned at the very top. Number One. She'd done it. Somehow Katie had lasted longer than any of the girls before her, including what Ditch considered to be the invincible (to a point) Daisy. The successful ascent to the top of the leader board had been enough for Ditch to throw her a party. Katie wasn't interested in a party, but Ditch insisted, and he always got what he wanted.

Katie sat in the middle of the cellar away from the bed for the first time since she arrived. The harsh chains that had rubbed and torn at her skin for so long lay loose atop the tattered bed. The manky blood and pissed-stained crusty sheets rested on the bed undisturbed for once. It was the first time Katie had this view of the bed and it was weird, almost an outer-body experience. It felt like she was seeing herself in third person, except she wasn't there. She had strongly suspected that the only time she'd leave the bed would be in a body bag, but for the moment, that wasn't the case.

She stared at the shadowy wall beyond the bed. From her new vantage point it seemed impossible that Reaper could have positioned himself there, the gap between the bed and the wall was far too small. A foot or two at best. But there he still was, lurking in the shadows looking back at her from an equal eye level. His hideous teeth shaped in a sinister grin shone from the darkness as he viewed the party. Katie looked away from Reaper and the bed when she received a sharp violent slap across the face. Ditch had warned her before about 'spacing out.' He'd gone to all the trouble of throwing her a party and she needed to fucking appreciate it, he'd repeatedly growled at her.

Despite being away from the bed chains Katie was still tied up. Not to the extremes of the bed, but Ditch had taken some precaution. Her legs were tightly bound by rope around the bottom of the stool, but her arms were free. Ditch had chosen not to tie her arms behind her back so he could enjoy his new handiwork. After Katie had shown signs of surviving the missing eye and ear that he'd badly stitched up he decided to help himself to a couple of fingers too. He got bored easily.

After taking far too long determining what weapon to use, Ditch had what he'd consider an epiphany and used his fucking teeth instead. It turned out biting someone's fingers off was a lot harder than the movies had made out. He'd taken for granted how much of the work saws and blades do, and just how difficult it was to chomp through bone, but he was intent on making it happen. Katie screamed the whole time but for once hadn't passed out. It took an hour but eventually, he managed to chew two fingers off before his jaw started to seriously ache and he had to stop.

Ditch had stapled together the remains of the fingers using the leftover flapping skin that he hadn't chewed off. It looked messy and grim, but that was the way he liked it.

Katie less so. Along with chewing off several of her fingers, he'd also changed her once again. The soiled revealing cheerleader uniform had been replaced with a fresh new slutty French maid outfit. That too was looking a lot worse for wear already but was still a big improvement on everything she'd worn previous. This was still at least identifiable.

Katie hadn't put up a struggle this time. She had nothing left to fight him with and was still not talking. He gave her a bunch of slaps and raped her anyway because that was the type of bastard he was, but she just let it happen, the fight left in her had evaporated. Ditch just wanted her to die now as she wasn't fun anymore and even fucking her had become a bit of a bore. He wasn't used to girls surviving this long after he'd broken them so hoped this party would be the straw that broke the camel's back. If not maybe he'd actually break her back because she was acting like a right fucking downer.

The small party consisted of just the two of them, or three if you counted Reaper skulking in the background, but he wasn't invited. Katie sat tied to the chair in the middle of the room dressed in her French maid's outfit with a pointy green party hat hanging from the side of her head. At this stage Ditch had largely ripped out most of her hair so the hat hid several of Katie's bald patches. The little that did remain of her previously beautiful hair looked thin and damaged and ready to fall out all by itself. He'd hung a congratulatory banner to the cellar ceiling over the leader board. Not that Katie gave a shit about being number one, Ditch had just hung it to annoy her. Any chance to piss her off he took without fail.

Sitting opposite her Ditch was wearing a new boiler suit, a grey one. He'd been thinking about adding to his collection for a while and now seemed a memorable time to splurge on a new outfit. He wouldn't forget the day the record was broken, so why not celebrate it? But it was as much Katie's party and day as his own, so he'd brought her a present too. It rested ominously beside his own stool crudely wrapped in black paper with far too much tape circled around it. Ditch didn't have a fucking clue how to do those neat folded corner things and wasn't about to try. The bitch should just be grateful she'd gotten anything at all, none of the other girls had.

Along with the party hat and present, there was also a takeaway and cake. Ditch had briefly considered making some party food, especially as it might bring back memories of him horrifically killing her boyfriend, but he was too lazy for that so just brought a bucket of chicken instead. It was cold by the time he got back to the cellar but he didn't care. The cake he'd brought from a supermarket like it was a completely normal thing to do, had *congratulations* on it and was probably meant for graduating or getting engaged but fuck it! Not his fault the supermarket didn't sell cakes commemorating lasting three and a half weeks being tortured, brutalised, and abused in a gloomy cellar.

Ditch always felt odd going out in public to places like the supermarket. He wasn't afraid of getting caught and arrested as he'd never seen a description of himself in the papers after the girls had gone missing. It was more that he'd largely withdrawn from the world and things like doing the weekly shopping or filling his pick-up with petrol now felt alien to him. It was the kind of shit people who don't have naked girls missing body parts tied up in their cellars did. But a guy's got to eat no matter how fucked up their lifestyle.

He cut a slice of cake using the same knife that had recently scared Katie's legs so badly, and she could still see some of the stained blood on the knife where he hadn't cleaned it afterwards. As meticulous as Ditch may have been with his boiler suits and the leader board the same level of cleanliness did not apply to the weapons and tools within the cellar. He liked to leave little reminders on those. A blacklight would freak the fuck out if it was aimed at the weapons table or the bed for that matter. Ditch placed the cake in Katie's hand, the one with the two fingers missing. God, he loved his life, he thought with a smirk when he could see her already struggling to hold it.

The creamy cake slid from Katie's mangled fingers. What was left of her claw-like hand couldn't grasp the soft cake and she hadn't tried anyway. She had stopped eyeballing Reaper after Ditch's slap but was now staring straight past Ditch instead. Not at anything in particular, she just looked kind of zoned out, but she wasn't. In her head, Katie was scheming. This had to be her only chance to do something, anything, she thought. She knew she'd never be in a better position than this, so to speak, and had to do something. Trying to plan her escape meant she hadn't been paying attention to Ditch once again and hadn't even realised he'd placed the cake in her hand.

Ditch cracked Katie across the mouth breaking yet another tooth with the impact of the punch. By this point they'd started looking so rotten and unhealthy that it hadn't surprised Katie to see another fly out, her mouth was starting to look as sparse as her hair. Katie rocked back on the stool from the force of the punch as it eventually tipped and sent her landing hard on her side as the chair tipped sideways. The pain of the fall felt incredibly minor whereas a month ago that would have hurt. She was numb to it now. It's amazing what the human body and mind could get used to.

"You ungrateful fucking bitch," Ditch grinned not actually remotely pissed at her dropping the cake. He knew it would happen, had wanted it too.

"Lick it up," he commanded as he stood and stepped in the cake making it squelch under his heavy boot. Katie surveyed the fallen cream cake spread across the floor from her position on the deck. It had landed on the unremovable stain because, of course, it had. Ditch planned all these things. His mind was a constant hive of activity as he worked out new ways to break her, this was all a giant game to him. No way was he going to ease off the mental and physical torture just because she'd topped the leader board, not even during a so-called party to celebrate her survival. For him this was just another opportunity to fuck with her and she knew it.

Katie scooted towards the fallen cake and reached for it with her better hand. Ditch instantly stamped down on her fingers. "You don't get to use your hands," he cruelly laughed. "You're an animal. Eat like one," he added, eager to see whether she would. Katie obliged. It didn't matter at this point. Maybe during the first week or two she'd have put up a fight and her pride would have been hurt but that mentality was long gone. She licked up the cake with her dry blister ridden tongue without hesitation. The cake was the first nice thing she'd had since she got here even though the five second rule had long passed, but she was in no condition to enjoy it. If anything it reminded her of the life she no longer had.

Ditch poked his boot in Katie's face showing remnants of cake stuck between the treads. He'd clearly stepped in plenty of mud or shit too judging by the state of the sole but that was all part of the fun. "You missed some," he announced. Katie didn't dither as she remained obedient and licked the cake from the bottom of this filthy boot much to Ditch's delight. "Greedy bitch," he spat at Katie while kicking her in the face. It wasn't enough to send another tooth flying as he had to be careful not to break her neck, but it still stung. Everything he ever did to her hurt whether she still showed it or not.

"Look at you," Ditch laughed. "Pathetic." He lifted her stool from the floor with the ropes tied around her legs still holding. "How on Earth have you lasted the longest?" He asked, half wanting her to answer. She didn't. "How has some pitiful creature that licks cake and dog shit from my boot outlasted all these other bitches?" He again asked wanting an answer while he pointed at the leader board. Once again Katie reminded silent. Ditch shook his head in mock astonishment at her great achievement.

He smiled at Katie. It wasn't rare for him to smile at her but Katie knew it was always a bad sign. Shit was always about to go down whenever he genuinely smiled at her, it always led to a supreme act of cruelty.

"Joking aside," he stated with a slightly more serious tone and no irony that nothing he'd ever done felt like a joke to Katie. "I've got a present for you," he again smiled. It was an even creepier smile than normal, Katie observed. Again not a good sign. "I will let you know in advance it's not the key to the door," he laughed. "I don't want to give you false hope," he added, "but it is a genuine gift from the heart."

Ditch sat back down and reached for the present waiting beside his stool. It looked heavy in his hand as he picked it up and Katie thought she heard a slight slushing sound but couldn't be certain.

"It really is amazing you've lasted this long," he told her looking at the extent of the damage he'd caused. The missing fingers and toes. The burnt, melted, and scarred body. The ripped-out eye and ear. The broken nose, cheek, and teeth. The infections spreading across all the badly healed wounds. She smelt of death. Looked like death. Had been near death constantly for several weeks yet still sat in front of him breathing. It was a truly remarkable achievement whether she felt like celebrating it or not.

Ditch leant towards Katie and handed her the present. This time he was careful to place it in her better hand and make sure she had a firm grip of it with the mangled hand too. He didn't want her to drop this. He needed her to open it and see the macabre horrors that waited inside…

… Instead the moment it rested in her hand she smashed it over his fucking head.

Death

The heavy glass jar hidden under the loose black wrapping paper shattered upon impact as water from within the jar cascaded to the floor. One of Ditch's hands remained alongside Katie's after gifting her the present while his other shot upwards towards the impact. He tightly held the top of his head unaware whether the wetness flowing from his forehead came from the water in the jar or if the bitch had busted him open. As the water dripping from his forehead turned red he knew it was a bit of both.

Before he could angrily react Katie flung her head forward and sunk what remained of her jagged rotten teeth into his present-giving hand. She bit him like a wild cat and doubled down by throwing her head around all over the place trying to tear his fucking hand off. She was a rabid dog that wouldn't let go of her victim no matter how much Ditch tried to shake her off. The docile compliant girl that had sat in front of him taking all his shit moments earlier was gone. Katie was frothing from the mouth now as she tried her own version of biting his fingers clean off.

"You cunt! You fucking whore! You nasty fucking…" Ditch's shouts echoed around the cellar as Katie persisted feeling the pressure of her own teeth breaking but not wanting to stop. "Get the fuck off me!" he screamed as blood started trickling from his trapped fingers. Katie didn't hear a word of the insults, she was in her own little world, one much happier than she'd been in for weeks. In this world she wasn't the victim as she tore a chunk from Ditch's hand. His screeches penetrated the bubble she was in, but only because she allowed it. She wanted to hear Ditch in pain for once as the only screams she'd heard for weeks on end had been her own.

Ditch viciously punched Katie with his one free hand as he tried to loosen her grip on his fingers. He could feel more skin tearing under the pressure of her broken teeth, their extra sharpness ironically of his own doing as he'd chipped every single one of them over the weeks. She wasn't far off reaching bone as the pain intensified. Katie's eyes, or rather eye, had a satanic edge to it as for a brief moment her evil equalled his in its ferocity. She wanted to fucking rip him apart and feed him his remains, but this was his cellar, his domain, not hers.

Another punch knocked her head back and thankfully for Ditch she lost her grip on his hand after taking yet another chunk. The follow-through however sent him spiralling to the floor as he landed on the awaiting carpet of shattered glass. A big meaty shard slipped through his arm several other smaller fragments stuck into him further up the arm. More glass ripped and tore at the left side of his body as he struggled to back out of the mess. Out of instinct Ditch put his already chewed hand down to push himself clear of the glass only to make matters worse for himself as a second chunkier loose piece penetrated his palm. More screams resonated around the dank cellar as Ditch inspected the damage.

Ditch had managed to drag Katie down with him as he

fell but she didn't give a shit about broken glass, she'd endured much worse. Landing on a slathering of shattered glass causing some cuts and scrapes was child's play compared to what Ditch had subjected her to over the last three weeks. Hell, over the last few days alone she'd lost an eye and a couple of fingers so fuck that glass.

What did get Katie's attention though was the squish she felt when she landed. While Ditch was screaming like a little bitch trying to remove the big glass shard from his arm that was causing blood to spray all over the cellar - his blood for once - Katie investigated the noise. Much to her disgust, but not really her surprise, she saw her clawed-out eyeball squashed underneath her. That sick fuck had given it back to her as a present like some kind of morbid memorabilia of her time here. She also noticed her detached fingers and toes resting close by looking like a school of discoloured fish that had made the mistake of jumping out the bowl. Her fucking ear lay amongst the mess as well completing Ditch's collection of greatest hits.

Just past the severed fingers and toes was the rest of the cake, but that wasn't what interested Katie. What she was interested in was the knife still sticking from the cake that Ditch had jammed in after cutting her a slice. She wasn't within reach of the knife but her arms were free and the ropes around her legs had loosened after the fall. She had two options while Ditch was still dicking around trying to get the glass out of his arm like a fucking baby. She could crawl through the glass and quickly get to the knife, or she could untie herself and go round the glass to get the knife while also having her legs free.

The chance for more freedom felt overwhelming but scrambling through the glass was the quicker option. Before she made a single movement forward Ditch booted her in the stomach in a fit of rage while still trying to pick the glass from his skin and unleashing all manner of insults on her. The kick spun Katie around, changing her decision as Ditch could no longer see what she was up to and the opportunity to untie herself came begging. While he continued to pick all the little pieces of glass from his arm and stare at the big fucker still embedded in his hand Katie began to untie her feet. The rope had loosened in the flurry of activity so despite having to do it one handed she got both legs free a lot quicker than she'd imagined.

Wasting no time Katie tried climbing to her feet but she hadn't used her legs in weeks and they were in a much worse state than the last time she had. She instantly fell the moment she stood reminding Ditch of her presence, but he didn't clock her untied legs. Katie squirming harmlessly around on the floor was the least of his worries as he continued to pluck the glass fragments from his arm. Katie fell forward again on her second attempt to stand but this fall left her within arm's reach of the knife.

Ditch looked down confused for a second as Katie lay stretching for the cake. If the whore wanted more cake then all she had to do was ask, he thought. Fuck, the punishment she was going to receive for all this wasn't worth any amount of cake, let alone the cheap dry store brought shit. But then he noticed what she was really going for as her one reasonable good hand wrapped around the handle of the blade he'd cockily left sticking from the congratulatory cake.

"You bitch," Ditch bellowed as he kicked forward trying to take Katie's head clean from her shoulders. But he didn't connect with her formerly pretty, but now devastated face, instead she leant to the side and stabbed at his foot as it came back down. "AWWW," Ditch cried out as the knife cut above his boot slicing his shin and drawing a new round of blood. Between the nasty cut on his forehead, the blood pissing from his arm, the glass stuck though his palm, and now his fucking leg leaking with the warm crimson too, he was beginning to imitate one of his victims.

This time Katie did somehow manage to get to her unsteady feet but she didn't get far. Ditch had stopped acting like a pussy as he removed the glass from his palm and entered full rage mode. He came towards her already swinging his dangerous fist with the intent of knocking the bitch out over and over again. Katie aimed the knife at him but he easily punched it from her grip despite his hand being a chewed up state with chunks missing from his fingers and now a hole in the middle caused by the glass. Ditch hadn't realised there was a big see-through hole in his hand when he'd curled his fist up, adrenaline at being stabbed had taken over, but now his hand hurt like hell. It was pain the likes of which he'd never felt before. He used to love saying that to his victims, but now was experiencing it himself. Fuck it, he had a second hand.

Ditch backhanded Katie to the floor with his own one good hand. Her fragile and beaten body was unable to absorb the blow regardless of how pumped she felt and how desperately she needed to get away from him. He fell to his knees mounting Katie where she landed and trapping her against the ground. Katie dug her three remaining fingers into one of the larger cuts on his side eliciting a yelp from Ditch but a swift headbutt to Katie's face put an end to that nonsense.

"You worthless cunt," he screamed, followed by twenty more uses of the word. All the time he pummelled her face bursting open the little that was left of her nose and taking another couple of teeth. The stitches in her removed eye came loose and the swelling around them began to bleed as another heavy punch broke her orbital bone. Blood poured from her cheek as that wound reopened and her whole face started to feel like it was coming loose as she heard the crunch of more bones breaking.

Katie tried to protect herself the best she could but her mangled weakened hands offered little in defence. Each punch reverberated around her body making what was left of her teeth tingle and the remaining toes stiffen. He stopped hitting her but only to put his mauled fingers around her neck once again forgetting about the hole in his hand as he used both to strangle Katie. All he saw was red. He couldn't believe the shit this cunt had pulled, he was a fucking mess. Him! That was not acceptable.

He spat at her several times as he foamed from the mouth. It was Ditch's turn to look and act like a mad dog.

His grip around her neck didn't relax as Katie's life began to fade away. Her hope of revenge had half succeeded, she may not have got to kill the murderous rapist bastard, but she'd fucking hurt him. She'd left her mark. Sure, she'll become the new unremovable stain story that he told future girls, but she had drawn more than just a little blood. She'd shown him to be weak. She had let all the other girls after her know that he wasn't untouchable. She knew he'd make a mistake again one day and another girl inspired by Katie would take a chance herself and have the pleasure of ending his wicked life.

With that thought Katie briefly smiled, something that Ditch did not react well too as his grip tightened, which in turn only made Katie's smile grow. He was going to lose twice today. Not only had she scarred and maimed his ass, she was going to rob him of his jerk off moment as well. She could see the murderous intent in Ditch's eyes, he'd lost all track of reason. He squeezed her throat tighter as Katie felt the last breaths failing. He was on the verge on killing her.

There would be no great victory for him, no whack off moment. No leering at her from his dominant position knowing that she'd given up, that he'd broken her. He hadn't broken her. She'd broken him. She'd won. Fuck you Ditch, you lose, Katie would have told him if she could get any words to escape her mouth. She couldn't, but she knew he'd know soon enough. Once the rage had settled he would have nothing left of this experience other than a bunch of nasty scars to forever remind him of his defeat.

Reaper may have been an asshole for saying it but he was right. Robbing Ditch of his moment did feel like a victory. It was just a shame it had to come at the expense of her own life. Katie's eyes rolled back in her head, her body couldn't fight anymore. Her last breath had already passed as she lay dead on the cellar floor. Katie had beat Ditch, even if it had cost her life.

Katie's First Day

It had been seven weeks since Ditch last brought a girl home. The last girl Esther had lasted eleven gruelling days in total in which Ditch had pulled a different tooth from her mouth every day and carved his name into her stomach along with the words 'property of.' He'd also taken to pissing on the poor girl on a daily basis in an attempt to bring her out of her shell. What his reasoning was behind that theory not even Ditch knew, he just thought it was fucking hilarious and really enjoyed doing it. It disgusted Esther more than the teeth pulling, so naturally, that just encouraged him to continue doing it.

But the constant pissing for nearly two weeks had left a foul smell lingering in the cellar. Not that it smelt of pine cones and lavender beforehand, but the reek of stale piss was making even Ditch's eyes water. After Esther finally gave in and died like a good little slut with Ditch's cock resting on her big bruised tits above the scrawled words on her stomach he went about giving the place a bit of a spring clean.

He was never going to get the place smelling pleasant with the amount of death that had come through its door, and the large black stain on the floor was never going to scrub out, but he could at least get it into a state where he didn't have to wear a mask. While a gas mask might protect him from the smell and help scare the shit out of the girls, he liked them seeing his face. Hiding behind a mask may have given them the illusion that one day he would let them go, whereas seeing his face sent a whole different message. He didn't want to give them false hope. He wanted them to know they were doomed from the moment he took them. Ditch was an honest guy like that.

With the place having a somewhat fresher smell, i.e not piss, he knew the day had come to bring home a fresh bitch. The taste and smell of Esther had drifted away and a new journey awaited. While her corpse was still decomposing in his home-made cemetery Ditch made plans for her replacement. He'd been spying on a girl several hundred miles away for a few weeks now, taking regular trips to her hometown. He always liked to pick his victims at vast distances from both his home and the last girl he snatched, making it impossible for any law enforcement to track him. This approach had served him well down the years with the missing girls' cases rarely being linked to one another.

This girl's name was Mandy and she was an absolute fucking beaut. From what he could tell she had a right mouth on her too, the sort he couldn't wait to try and shut up. Esther really had been a little too shy for his liking especially as the girl before her lasted less than a day or two. He needed a new girl who would pose a bit more of a challenge. Someone who wouldn't wilt at his very presence. He wanted to earn that reaction, not start with it, and Mandy seemed to be a strong-willed mouthy cunt that would fit the bill perfectly.

Unfortunately for Ditch, the kidnapping didn't go to plan in the slightest and by the end of the attempt Mandy was on a plane to fuck knows where completely unaware of how close she'd come to her death. Ditch had never failed to grab a girl before and the aura of defeat was following him on the long trip back home. He felt disgusted with himself and unsure when the next victim would be. He normally didn't wait this long between girls but had decided this one would be worth the extra wait, especially to give the cellar a bit of a dusting. That now felt like a massive miscalculation...

...Until he saw a beat-up old Pontiac Fiero parked in a hillside lay-by with an attractive couple drinking wine on its roof. He had no interest in the guy, that wasn't his thing, but the girl looked beautiful in the moonlight, and taking her was a sure-fire way to boost his ego and rid himself of the frustrating day. So he did.

*

The heavy cellar door swung open and Katie was carelessly thrown inside. The landing on the concrete cellar floor woke her from her drug-induced daze but she hadn't the slightest idea where she was. Katie could remember little bits of what had happened in the last few hours but most of it had been a blur. A horrible nightmarish blur that she truly hoped against all hope was the worse dream ever conceived. The lump forming on her bloody head, and her jaw awkwardly clicking out of place, was proof that it was all real.

Her boyfriend had been brutally murdered and his killer had kidnapped her, that's what she had awoken to. He'd taken her to some dingy cellar fuck knows where and she was utterly helpless to do anything about it. Whatever he had jabbed her with was starting to wear off but Katie already knew that it was a bad thing, she didn't want to feel what was coming. One look around the room told her only pain lay in her future, and she started to remember him telling her so back on the hillside. The stench of death in the room was rotten to the core despite there being a hint of cleaning products, the murderous smell had seeped into absolutely everything and no amount of disinfectant could mask that.

Ditch grabbed Katie by the hair and dragged her kicking and screaming to a bed on the far side of the room, the furthest she could possibly be from the door. Despite the desperate situation, and her frantic attempts, she couldn't free herself from his grasp or stop him from tightening the restraints around her body. Before she knew it both her arms and legs were strapped and chained and she was lying flat and vulnerable on an uncomfortable bed. In a blink of an eye whatever possible last gasp chance of freedom she believed she might have had already been snatched away.

Ditch introduced himself to Katie by grunting his name like he was just saying a random word. Before she had a chance to plead her case and beg to be let go he violently ripped her knickers from under her dress so that they tore and he didn't have to go through the hassle of unchaining her. Ditch smelt the underwear before tossing them to one side while Katie screamed for help at the top of her lungs already realising pleading wasn't going to achieve anything.

A well-placed punch to the gut stopped the screaming and started a scramble for breath instead. "You can cut that shit out right away," he coldly told her. "Ain't no one going to hear you here. You're all mine." Katie tried catching her breath but the shock of being hit yet again made it hard. Tears streamed down her face as her cheeks turned red, and she was close to a full-blown panic attack, something she hadn't experienced since sitting her exams all those years ago.

"Now let me tell you how it's going to be," Ditch began as though it was her first day at a new job. "I'm going to torture you in every way I know how, and you're going to take it until you can't handle anymore." Katie half paid attention and half couldn't understand what the fuck had happened while she continued to struggle for breath. How had her lovely evening with Ryan taken such a drastic turn? What the hell was going on? How could Ryan really be dead? And how the unholy-fuck was she chained up in some madman's torture chamber?

Ditch noticed her not paying attention so he left her zoned out on the bed for the moment while he made his way to the tool table. He grabbed a pair of pliers thinking he'd start off simple, there would be plenty of time for the more fun stuff. With Katie still in a daze, he grabbed her dislocated jaw and prised her mouth open wrapping the pliers around one of her front teeth. That got her attention. He continued his sermon.

"When you can't take it anymore, feel free to give up and die like the worthless whore you are." He looked back towards a whiteboard at the opposite end of the room. "In the meantime let's see how well you do compared to all the other bitches." He yanked the tooth from her mouth sending Katie into a screaming fit as blood poured from her gum. He gave her another slap to try and shut her the fuck up but Katie was too far gone in the moment to register it.

Ditch looked down at her already pleased with his work. God it felt good to have a woman around the place again, it had been far too long since Esther and he promised himself at that moment never to have such a big gap again. It would be a risk snatching more girls and doing less research, but from now on he thought a two to three week gap between bitches would be more than adequate. It was a risk he was willing to take in order to not have to wait so long between hearing the delightful sounds of new screams.

"Judging by your whining I'll give you a couple of days at best. But I sincerely hope you surprise me." Ditch continued his stare at the pitiful creature beneath him wondering if she'd be any fun at all, or whether killing her boyfriend in front of her had already broken her spirit. Only one way to find out. Either way at the end of her sorry life he'd have earned that glorious buzz knowing he'd broken another girl so much that they'd rather waste away and die than face him anymore.

Fear The Reaper

"Shit." Ditch looked perplexed at Katie's dead body as she lay strangled to death on the cold cellar floor amongst broken glass and ruined cake. The red mist of anger that had inhabited his mind had lifted, all that remained was the results of his violent rage. "Shit. Shit. Shit. Shit." Ditch gawked at Katie willing her to draw another breath. She didn't. "Fuck!" A different kind of panic ran through his head, a realisation he'd just fucked himself. This wasn't how it was meant to end. He'd broken his own rules and cost himself his prize. "You fucking cunt!" He screamed at the body like it was her fault she'd been strangled to death at his hands.

Ditch kneeled down beside the body being careful not to stab himself with another shard of broken glass. Why on earth had he bought such a big heavy jar for something as tiny as an eye, an ear, and a couple of fingers and toes? He thought it would be funny, that it would look like one of those mutant alien foetus-type jars you saw in horror movies or at freak shows. He was all ready to burst out laughing and point at her pathetic dumbstruck face but Katie had other ideas. Ditch didn't even think her brain was working anymore, but in hindsight, he guessed that was her plan. Well now she was dead so how'd that work out for her, he thought?

The answer was probably pretty well. She'd escaped his torture and stopped him from making her take her own life while also preventing him from getting the moment he oh so craved. Well, fuck that. Ditch wove his nibbled fingers together and placed them over Katie's starved chest. He'd never tried to bring a victim back to life before as it kind of defied the whole point of what he was doing. He'd taken them near death so many times that it was always a possibility, but normally something clicked in his brain at the exact moment it needed to and made him exercise the right amount of last-second restraint. Not this time though. This time he'd gone all the way and killed the bitch robbing himself of the pleasures he sought.

Ditch began performing CPR. He wasn't too concerned about cracking a rib, several were already broken and he didn't need her alive for long. Just enough for Katie to willingly fade from existence while he came over her dying, and then dead, body. He pressed down hard and fast not really sure how he was meant to perform this. It was one of those things he was taught thirty-plus years ago and instantly forgot. How the fuck were people meant to remember such trivial things as how to bring another person back to life?

He blew in her mouth a couple of times because he remembered something about doing that but couldn't recall exactly how it worked, just that it was part of the resuscitation process. He just needed her to fucking breath again, why was that so complicated? This wasn't how it was meant to end, especially after lasting this long. He wanted that same high he felt when the former champ Daisy finally succumb. That same buzz he got when he chopped her tongue out and sewed her mouth shut and hacked her hands off so she had no way to fight back and finally curled up and died after being seemingly unbreakable. He wanted that feeling again, with Katie, and had felt so close to achieving it. Fuck he thought he was going to get it today. Today was the day she was going to die, he'd felt it in every fibre of his being, and he was right, but not like this.

"Don't you fucking ruin this for me!" He yelled in her face giving her a slap in the process, but Katie's fight was over. She showed no signs of life as Ditch continued to punch down on her chest hoping that he could hit her hard enough to bring the air back. Fuck if he knews he was just getting desperate as Katie lay there with an annoying smile still etched on her face. Ditch hadn't noticed the smile remained at first but now it was even more motivation to bring her back, he wanted to wipe that stupid fucking grin off her face and watch her die properly this time. At her own hands, not his.

Reaper watched from beside Ditch. He'd made his way forward when Katie took her last breath but now patiently waited for Ditch to give up his feeble attempts to bring her back. Reaper had waited long enough to collect Katie's soul so another minute wouldn't hurt. He'd watched the whole incident unfold like he was at the theatre and it had been quite the show. For the briefest of moments he thought there would be a massive twist and Katie would somehow triumph, especially when she made it to the knife, but no-one escapes Ditch. Although by his own reckoning, and the advice he'd given her, she was still victorious in the end.

Ditch gave up the CPR and kicked Katie's prone body as he stood. "Fuck!" He shouted once again still enraged at the turn of events. What a waste of three weeks. Ditch bent down and ripped a strip from Katie's French maid's outfit and wrapped it around the gaping hole in his bloody palm and gnawed fingers. Normally he had plenty of rags on his person but hadn't added any to the new boiler suit yet which was now covered in more of his own blood than hers. The rare purchase had already been forever tainted. Another fucking waste. The open wound on his palm stung like hell and he definitely needed to go to the hospital to get it seen to, but that would have to wait. For the moment he was still fuming and needed to calm down.

He reluctantly strolled to the leader board leaving Katie dead on the floor. His eyes fell on the Polaroid of her at the top. This was meant to be a good day, a day to torture her even more. To revel in her 'success' by bringing even more unbearable pain, more brutality, more mental anguish than she could possibly handle. In a way he'd done the first part of that, but not the right way. Killing her was not how he did business. Ditch lowered his head, disappointed in himself. Something he rarely felt within the realm of the cellar.

He really had been looking forward to watching Katie permanently submit. She'd put up such a good fight, a most unexpected one after her first few whiny days. His cock tingled at how good the reward would have felt, how orgasmic and fulfilling it would have been when she finally accepted death and let herself go. "Fuck," he said once more but without the rage behind it this time.

Ditch looked back at Katie's body, still on the floor. He considered trying to bring her back once again but had to admit defeat. There was a lesson to learn here, and he'd learn it just like he learnt from the whole nail gun incident with a previous girl. Ditch was good at trial and error. If he ever found himself in such a situation again he knew he'd handle it better, he'd find a way to regain his composure. Losing his cool had lost him the ultimate buzz and that could never happen again. Still, even with her deformed face and mangled body, she looked pretty fucking appealing lying there dead in her bloody ripped maid's outfit, Ditch thought. Maybe he could still fuck her corpse? Salvage something from all of this. His eyes returned to the leader board as he considered the new morbid option already thinking he might just go ahead with it.

Reaper knelt beside Katie giving her a friendly smile to suggest she'd done well, good for her taking his advice and goading Ditch into strangling her to death. He held his scythe tightly in his left hand standing it perfectly upright and still like an altar while he leant over her with his right hand. He pressed the hand against her chest and spread his bony fingers the circumference of her heart as the tips began to turn glow and he began the process of removing her soul. He closed his eyes to focus his energy in order to start the undertaking but as he did Katie's own eyes sprang open. A gasp of breath escaped her still somehow alive body.

Reaper looked shocked as Katie grabbed the handle of the scythe and ran it across his bony throat in one quick as a flash movement. A waterfall of black liquid cascaded from the cut bone splashing down on Katie and drenching her face. Reaper tried to clasp his hands around the ghastly wound but couldn't stop the flow of the blacker than black life force. He looked at Katie one last time with an expression that suggested betrayal, a wonderment at how she could have done this to him, but Katie didn't give a shit. He'd known she didn't see him as innocent in all of this, and slicing his bony fucking throat open was the least he deserved in her eyes.

His dead eyes appeared even more dead as they somehow rocked back in his large eye socket as he collapsed to the floor. The blood(?) that Katie didn't even know Reaper contained worked like a bucket of ice water being thrown over her as it had cascaded down. It had jolted her back into some kind of clear thinking after moments beforehand being dazed and practically dead. Katie wasn't entirely sure why she was alive, but the taste of Ditch in her mouth and a few more broken ribs gave her a possible clue as to how.

Whatever the reason it didn't matter. She was alive, and more importantly to Katie, Ditch was unaware of this fact and currently had his back turned to her. Her eyes scanned the cellar as she spotted the knife lying amongst glass, blood, and cake, but better options were just above her as Katie turned her head towards the weapons table. She couldn't see what lay on top from her position on the floor but that sick fuck had used enough of the table's content for Katie to have a pretty good idea of the options available…

… But then she spotted the bloodstained heavy-duty pipe wrench resting against the side of the table. The very same wrench he'd use to beat Ryan to a gooey pulp. The one that was briefly home to her eye before that sick bastard stuck it in a jar and tried giving it back to her as a present. Bet he regretted that now, Katie briefly thought. The wrench was within close proximity to her too. She looked towards Ditch who still had his back turned to her while he dicked around with the leader board. No doubt he was drawing a line though her name to officially finalise her death, Katie reasoned. How little he knew.

Katie dragged herself towards the wrench leaving a trail of black and red blood to mark her progress. Her broken ribs and destroyed body made every breath a miracle and she could barely see out of what was left of her one remaining eye. If Ditch admired her fight before today her stock was most definitely on the rise. She reached for the pipe wrench and took the handle with her better hand using the long metal tool to aid her ascent as she tried once again to stand. Katie reached her feet but needed the wrench as a crutch just as much as she needed it as a weapon, a fair compromise considering she was lying on the floor dead moments ago.

Using the mammoth wrench that she could barely hold as a walking stick sent an echo throughout the near-silent cellar. Ditch's heavy breathing and swearing had provided cover for her movement so far but there was no way he wasn't going to hear the sound of metal against concrete. It didn't matter, Katie didn't have much ground to cover, which was a good because her unusable mutilated legs were about to give out.

Ditch stopped what he was doing at the clang of the metal wrench on the floor. At first he thought the wrench had fallen over. A reasonable thing to think considering the mess he and that cunt had made of the cellar during their fight, but the second clang that followed was definitely odd. He turned in time to see Katie standing behind him drenched in some kind of thick black liquid with the white of her one eye gleaming through the gunk. That fucking smile that had remained after she perished was still on her face too.

WHACK.

Katie swung the bloodstained pipe wrench at Ditch's head with a strength she didn't know she had. A stored up strength that had been powered by all the abuse and torment she'd suffered at the hands of Ditch for the last three weeks. It was a one-time deal, and this was that time. The metal wrench connected solidly on the bottom of Ditch's jaw, right on the button. She knocked him the fuck out.

Ditch

Ditch's eyes slowly opened focusing on an unfamiliar sight above him - the cellar roof. Before he had time to comprehend what exactly that meant pain shot through several parts of his body. He tried reaching for his jaw first, the epicentre of where the most recent pain began, but a chain prevented his hand from moving. "What the fuck?" He tried to mumble but the words were lost before they came out of his mouth as his broken jaw didn't comply, it hung loosely from the bottom of his face leaving his mouth permanently open. But Ditch hadn't fully registered that yet.

His attention turned to his legs as he tried sitting, but they too were tightly bound. His whole body was at full stretch with very little give. Ditch's main ability for movement consisted of being able to nod and twist his head, but that just confused him further when he looked towards the cellar door now fully realising he was chained to the decrepit bed. Lying in the middle of the cellar was what appeared to be a male body. 'Where the fuck had he come from?' was the first thought that entered Ditch's mind, closely followed by, is that his skull? The body was draped in a cloak lying in a pool of what appeared to be thick black blood with just his dull skeleton head showing and a discarded scythe resting by his side.

Ditch rattled the chains as he tugged with all his might to get free but these chains were built to last. He should know. His left arm gave up first in the attempt. A glance to the arm, which was all he could manage, showed it was torn to shreds. He remembered a large glass shard stuck to it, and plucking out a bunch of smaller pieces, but the injury had evolved from that. He was pretty certain he could see bone and veins however his eyes refused to focus on the disgusting sight. Ditch tried recoiling away from the mess, but the chains prevented him. With the shoe on the other foot that would have made him laugh for days but he no longer saw the funny side.

He tried screaming to be released but the shouts didn't escape his mouth. Instead they evoked more pain from his jaw which he now realised was broken as he could see it hanging on the edge of his periphery. The sight induced more panic as he tried in vain to pull himself free of the chains again, barring the aid of his left arm this time. All his jiggling around produced was soft laughter nearby. Ditch couldn't see the source, but there was only one possibility.

Ditch looked to the being on the floor and an image flashed in his head of Katie being covered in the same black blood holding his pipe wrench. Katie! Fuck, he thought, she was alive. She's the one that had done this to him. As if sensing Ditch's realisation, Katie spoke to him from below as she sat against the cold hard bed, "Your arm looked a mess so I tried amputating it for you." She let the words hang for a second, "but I gave up halfway."

He risked another glance at his arm and his first impression was correct as this time he forced his eyes to focus. It was a lot fucking worse than how he left it. Muscle and bone were showing throughout, along with his stretched and exposed tendons on full display. Several different saw marks ate into various parts of what was left of the arm, all different angles through an assortment of failed attempts to chop the fucking thing off. He probably could pull that arm free of the chains, but definitely not the way he'd intended. The thought and sight made him sick, but that just hurt his jaw as the puke dribbled from his loose mouth.

"I've put you on the board," Katie coldly told him, her tone factual rather than full of hate or satisfaction. Ditch tried looking downwards to see her but Katie's slumped position kept her out of view. Instead he looked towards his feet and saw the leader board had been moved across the room and was in plain view of him now that he was looking. A part of him wanted to rant at her and belittle her for daring to fuck around with the organisation of his cellar, but he was in no position to do that. It pissed him off royally though. Maybe this was Katie's way of playing mind games? Sure enough his name did sit at the bottom, 'Ditch, Day One.' While looking in that direction he noticed several removed toenails too. Bitch.

He tried asking Katie what she'd done to his feet but the words came out a bumbling mess like he was trying to talk with his mouth stuffed to the brim. Katie was able to guess at the question though knowing where she'd directed him and hearing another pang of suffering entering his voice. "Eye for an eye," she stated once again leaving a gap in the conversation before she finished, "but we'll get to that part," she told him as she began the slow process of getting to her feet.

A blinding light flashed before Ditch's eyes while he stared at the board, and his feet, trying to piece together what happened. He turned to the source of the light with his eyes blurred from the flash and saw Katie holding his Polaroid camera. Another fucking thing of his the bitch had touched. How dare she? She started shaking the picture while she stood before him lacking all the power Ditch had in a similar pose, but like him in that position, she was in control.

The girl looked like death even within Ditch's currently limited vision. There was barely anything left of her before he killed her, but now she looked a few stages on from even that. Her skin was a ghostly white with all the colour completely drained from her face and the black marks that had formed around her neck over the last three weeks had drastically darkened after the latest supposedly life-ending strangulation. Ditch wondered how the fuck she could possibly still be alive, especially as she was dead? That's when it suddenly occurred to him that he may have been responsible for bringing her back. Fucking stupid CPR.

Katie smugly, in Ditch's eyes, showed him the exposed picture. His face contorted in terror at his hideous appearance. His jaw looked like something from the Edvard Munch painting while she had also captured part of his arm that looked ready to fall right off. The bitch had broken his nose too and given him a black eye. He didn't know if that was from the initial wrench shot or whether she'd been pummelling him while he was out cold, but either way, he couldn't ask her in any coherent manner with his jaw hanging.

She pinned the Polaroid next to his name on the leader board and attempted a smile in his direction as Ditch's vision cleared. She barely had a tooth to speak of as her mouth looked like one of those hillbillies from a bad slasher flick. Black blood had seeped from the wound across her lost eye and her nose appeared to be missing after the final beating he gave her. The gap where her ear used to be had turned a nasty shade of multiple dark colours while the last few strands of hair she had left had fallen from her head.

Her maid's outfit was ripped exposing one of her blackened tits but she either didn't notice, or didn't care. Her arms looked bruised and weak and her missing fingers had become even more infected with black blood oozing from them too. Her legs looked like she'd survived a house fire and her feet were barely recognisable as feet. All in all there wasn't a single part of her now that looked anything remotely like the innocent girl Ditch had first brought to the cellar.

Katie's ugly appearance brought Ditch great joy only hours ago, but the unnerving expression on her disfigured face had taken the fun out of it. Now she looked like a creature that would haunt you in your nightmares rather than the pathetic beaten girl laughably on the verge of death as she licked his boot.

Ditch struggled for freedom again after taking in her

demonic face, but it wasn't happening. He'd installed these chains to last, doubly so after that cunt Jasmine tried to escape. He wasn't going anywhere and Katie's gummy warped smile knew it too. He wanted to shout all kinds of obscenities at her and finish the job he'd started but he was in no position to do either. Ditch was powerless for the first time in a long time. Not that he wanted to but he couldn't even plead his case for her letting him go, and there wasn't even the slightest chance she would.

Katie slowly made her way to the weapons table and picked up a saw having seemingly made her choice before she'd reached the table. She walked towards Ditch's lower body as he tried to scream at her to leave him alone. All he managed to do was gargle a little and Katie paid no attention to him anyway. She raised the bloody saw that she'd already used on his arm over his big toe and without any hesitation began to saw it off. Ditch thrashed his foot around trying to free it from the jagged blade but all that achieved was her nicking other parts of his foot too. She gave him a 'really?,' expression before continuing unperturbed by his pathetic non-wails as he was left with no choice but to let her cut.

After the toe came off Katie tossed it to the side and in a nonchalant manner moved to the big toe on his other foot repeating the same action. Ditch's muffled screams demanded to know what the fuck was going on and how she could possibly be alive but Katie didn't understand a word of it, and wouldn't have offered an explanation anyway. Exhausted, she cast the other toe aside and staggered back to the weapons table without acknowledging Ditch who was fucking apoplectic by this point, and he couldn't do a single thing about any of it.

Ditch's eyes followed her the whole way only stopping briefly to examine the body on the floor again. Who the fuck was that? His attention returned to Katie as she hovered over him with a screwdriver in hand. Ditch's murmured pleas were cut-off when Katie drove the screwdriver into his thigh. The stab didn't have much force behind it but it did the damage puncturing his leg. Katie's exhausted body lay prone on Ditch for a moment as she seemed momentarily out of energy.

He couldn't do anything about her temporary vulnerable state, couldn't even snatch her hair where she had none left. He tried jabbing his fingers in her face but the deformed mess was just out of his reach. Watching her she didn't appear to be breathing, and he couldn't feel the beats of her chest on his as she lay draped across him, but her eyes still stared towards his with pure hatred and disgust pouring from them. She lifted her head a little, the only real indication she was alive, as some energy seemed to return to her body. Ditch didn't know whether he was relieved or not. With her dead the suffering would stop, but no fucking way was he escaping these chains, and there was zero chance of ever being found.

As she slowly stood back up Katie slapped Ditch across the face mimicking what he often done to her. Despite mostly thinking about how much that screwdriver stab fucking hurt his brain did manage to process something else during the weak slap, her hand was cold. Not chilly, but absolutely freezing. What wasn't cold was the blow torch she used on him next. Katie seared the puncture wound she'd just created while also turning it to the gaping hole in the palm of his hand. "That should help," she told Ditch with a renewed energy in her voice and acting like she'd just finished lifesaving surgery.

"You're going to fucking pay for this," Ditch belched at her with none of the words sounding anything like they should. Katie wasn't listening anyway, and instead she pulled a big knife from the table, something far bigger than the one used to cut the cake. This looked like the sort of knife a survivalist would take to the jungle.

"I've been dreaming of doing this for three weeks," she told Ditch in her weakened voice as she poised the knife above his one good hand. It really was an absolute miracle she was standing, let alone being able to shit talk and torture him but Katie wasn't thinking about that, she was running on pure adrenaline and hatred. Ditch's eyes begged for mercy. Not a fucking chance.

Katie slit his wrist. Just one quick swipe with the horrible jagged knife and Ditch's veins were opened. The blood flow was a surprise even to Ditch despite how much he'd caused during his years torturing countless woman. He couldn't even cover the wound, all he could do was wail and watch as the blood exited his body at an alarming rate. Katie slit the wrist on the crippled arm too for good measure.

She stepped back and watched as the blood poured

from Ditch's wrists onto the disgusting bedsheets and leaked to the cellar floor. He watched in utter amazement and shock not knowing what else he could do at this point. His days were numbered, in fact he probably only had seconds left. He didn't try to beg or plea as Katie stood above him with the knife at the ready once more, instead he just observed as she plunged the huge commando knife through his heart delivering the final blow and exacting the revenge she had held on so long for. She wasn't going to play this game the same way he did, he was going to die at her hands, not his own.

Somehow still alive, Ditch looked up at Katie. She smiled at him. He could still somehow see her menacing smile. It morphed to a stupid grin as she could see from the expression on his pained face just how confused he was. Ditch didn't know whether to laugh or cry. Was he invincible? If so, that was news to him, potentially fucking cool news as well. Or had she tricked him in some way? Was it a retractable knife? No, that's stupid. Where would she get a retractable knife from, he thought. Plus that wouldn't explain the obvious and exceedingly agonising slit wrists and buckets of blood washed up on the floor from them, not to mention the searing pain exploding from heart, cut in half. What the fuck?

Katie didn't offer any explanation, she just continued to grin at him like she couldn't quite believe it herself. She could. She had a hunch after killing Reaper that this was a possibility, but had to know for sure. In for a penny, in for a pound, she thought as she put her experiment to the test and killed Ditch to see if he'd remained alive. Ditch was still struggling to determine whether this new turn of events was a good thing or a bad thing when Katie finally offered an answer.

She casually walked to the weapons table at her own slow methodical pace and retrieved a chainsaw he'd never got around to using. It felt awkward in her hands with her missing fingers making it difficult to grip but over time she knew she'd get more comfortable with it. She carefully carried the chainsaw towards Ditch's midsection as he began to realise his still being alive maybe wasn't for the best after all.

"You know what Ditch?" Katie said sounding tired but with a happy undertone in her voice as she revved the chainsaw up. She didn't complete her statement at first and instead ploughed the chainsaw into Ditch's stomach sending pieces of his internal organs flying in the air and covering both of them head to toe in his blood as it bit through his belly. Ditch's screams escaped even his broken jaw as he felt the chainsaw chewing up and spitting out his insides. Of all the pain he'd ever caused, which was a fucking lot, he'd never come close to delivering something like this.

Katie pulled the chainsaw away from the massive hole where his stomach once was and briefly turned it off as Ditch's screams intensified to levels she never reached. She carefully lowered the powered-down chainsaw just below his now missing stomach and cut a gap in Ditch's boiler suit exposing his limp shrivelled dick that had tried to climb back inside Ditch only to discover there wasn't an inside anymore. While turned off, the chainsaw had still taken a nasty chuck from his thigh as she cut through the suit. Oh well. She powered the chainsaw back up and let it rev over his cock for several seconds before she lowered it, chainsawing his dick clean off and ripping through his balls too. The previous worse pain ever of being chainsawed through the stomach had already been beaten, and Katie had plenty more ideas whirling around her brain.

"I think you have a real chance at breaking my record," Katie told him as Ditch's screams reverberated around the cellar as he remained very much alive.

The End.

BOOKS BY STEPHEN COOPER

Abby Vs The Splatploitation Brothers
Hillbilly Farm

Near Death

Printed in Great Britain
by Amazon